I0519508

JACK MARLIN, PRIVATE EYE: THE CASE OF THE BARBARY BLACKBIRD

A Modern-Day Penny Dreadful
set in San Francisco, California 1935

Original Story and Screenplay

by

Victoria Nelson

DREAMING SPIRES **PUBLICATIONS**

First Edition 2012

Copyright © 2005 Victoria Nelson

Reg. # PAu2-954-030

Jack Marlin, Private Eye: The Case of the Barbary Blackbird is the sole property of the author, Victoria Nelson, and is fully protected by copyright. With the exception of short quotations used for the purpose of academic research or instruction, no part of this publication may be reproduced, altered, or acted in public or private including public readings, radio, television, film, digital recording, and online broadcasts without permission of the author and payment of royalty. All inquiries concerning rights, royalties, licensing, merchandising, and permissions should be addressed to dreamingspirespublications@live.com.

Note: In addition to the script, there is available from the author a well-researched film production suggestion guide for use by animators, storyboard artists, directors and producers, detailing the appearance of authentic period places, modes of transportation, settings, clothing and characters.

ISBN: 0615567835
ISBN 13: 9780615567839

Cover Designed by: Kura Carpenter
Web: kuracarpenterdesign.blogspot.co.nz

INTRODUCTION

In a multidimensional universe, there is certainly room for myriads of spirits, and creation myths from the earliest times have affirmed their existence. We are instinctively drawn to apply these theories and in many cases relegate them to the level of sacred writing and art, and indeed we will continue to do so. When speaking of ethereal possibilities and especially with regard to the literary imagination there exists much more than just the probability of elves, dwarves, hobbits, angels, aliens, gnomes, pixies, indeed any ethereal creature including goblins, orcs and trolls living side by side with humans, whether now or in the past, on this planet or elsewhere, and why not? Who is to say what can and cannot exist in the invisible dimensions of this world and on the uncharted reaches of others? Similar to the sometimes controversial role of modern art, imaginative Literature and digital animation have brought to life beings and environments that assist in moving us beyond our self-imposed cognitive limits of what is possible.

Jack Marlin, Private Eye: The Case of the Barbary Blackbird is a tribute to the work of Raymond Chandler and to his creation, Philip Marlowe. The story takes place in the city of San Francisco and Muir Woods in 1935 during the Art Deco Era and provides an opportunity for the audience to experience an imaginative, historically accurate recreation of an architecturally, artistically and culturally unparalleled time in American history. America does have a rich and vibrant culture, and the Detective genre, *à la* Philip Marlowe, is quintessentially American. Raymond Chandler said of Marlowe,

> I may be wrong, but to me Marlowe is a character of some nobility, of scorching wit, sad but not defeated, lonely but never really sure of himself. He will at any time, because he is that sort of a man, meet any danger, since he thinks that is what he was created for,

and because he knows the corruption of his country can only be cured by men who are determined if necessary to sacrifice themselves to cure it.[1]

Such a character is needed today — a fallible hero, an everyday human being who seeks goodness for its own sake whether convenient or inconvenient.

With regard to storytelling there are five deplorable elements popularly accepted today as a mainstay of family entertainment. They are drivel, chaos, provocativeness, vulgarity and offensive innuendo, each of which can only serve to dehumanize children and adults alike. Examples of the application of these elements can be found in making an unjustified mockery of parents, teachers or civil authority figures, as well as mocking viable cultural customs and traditions such as good manners.

James Bond creator Ian Fleming at the conclusion of his last interview said,

> I'm very tired of this "kitchen sink" period. In fact, the boiled cabbage school bores me to tears. It isn't necessary to wallow in filth to know what filth is. Things go altogether too far when filth is viewed as beauty and obscenity becomes accepted communication. [. . .] We'll take any four-letter word without a flinch, and I suppose that those words will ultimately lose their shock, then their meaning. I think that they rather strike an attitude on the page, however, and I refuse to use them. On the other hand I'm glad to see a return to romantic writing — at least a swing toward it. The story with a beginning, a middle, and an end seems to be returning to favor, and this should be good for everyone.[2]

It is unconscionable to imagine that writers and filmmakers, as artists, could ever consider themselves so free as to identify as art and thrust onto the public any creation that degrades humanity or mocks that which can be considered sacred.

Although children possess the full range of human emotion and finer feeling, they do not always have the educational background or life experience to articulate these sentiments appropriately. As a result there are large numbers of young people today being suspected of having learning and/

or behavioral disorders when in fact they are merely lacking in cultural literacy. When Laurence Olivier as an anguished King Lear stands on that hillock in the rain and wind, drenched to the bone, waving his arms at the sky and yelling, "Blow winds, and crack your cheeks! Rage, blow! / You cataracts and hurricanoes . . ." (3.2.2), he is expressing a depth of human emotion that children can naturally identify with.

Rosemary Sutcliff, author of historical fiction, believed it was vital that her writing provide young people not only with the ability to use words to give shape and manageability to their thoughts and ideas, but most importantly to assist in the process of forming their conscience and influencing in some morally significant way the kind of persons they will become.[3]

In "A Defence of Penny Dreadfuls," G. K. Chesterton offers a brilliant rationale for the reading of narratives not always in keeping with society's prescribed norms for children and popularly undervalued and depicted as "vulgar" (lacking sophistication) or ignorant in the literary sense by saying that the Penny Dreadfuls such as "Dick Deadshot" are "not vulgar intrinsically," but are "the actual centre of a million flaming imaginations". Moreover, "it is we," says Chesterton, "who are the morbid exceptions . . . The vast mass of humanity, with their vast mass of idle books and idle words, have never doubted and never will doubt that courage is splendid, that fidelity is noble, that distressed ladies should be rescued, and vanquished enemies spared."[4]

In America, the hard-boiled language of the 1930's detective mystery/thriller, and especially the Chandleresque brand, is more than just a form of slang—it serves as an emotional and intellectual catharsis, and like the language of Shakespeare can provide a venue to emote and express ideas without resorting to the use of crude language. To defend the fallible hero and to emulate the good he or she represents is to hold on to the hope that in the end all will be right with the world because The Good, in spite of our limitations, will out.

NOTES

[1] Frank McShane, Ed. *Selected Letters of Raymond Chandler* (New York: A Delta Book, 1987) 452.

[2] Roy Newquist, "Ian Fleming's Last Interview" *Show* November 1964:91

[3] Victoria Nelson, "Rosemary Sutcliff's Arthurian Trilogy," *Saint Austin Review* December 2002:10.

[4] G. K. Chesterton, "A Defence of Penny Dreadfuls," (From *The Defendant* published in *The Wayfarer's Library* by J. M. Dent and Sons Ltd, London, 1901).

CAST IN ORDER OF APPEARANCE

1. JACK MARLIN, gnome detective

2. B.C. (BUTTERCUP), gnome daughter of PHIL

3. PARKS, gnome chief of police

4. SHERWOOD (SHERRY), squirrel

5. CLAUDINE, female calico alley cat

6. CHESTER, male pug dog, companion to CLAUDINE

7. AARON, gnome member of the Barbary Blackbird gang

8. RUFE, gnome member of the Barbary Blackbird gang

9. DANNY, gnome member of the Barbary Blackbird gang

10. JASE, gnome member of the Barbary Blackbird gang

11. TOBY, gnome member of the Barbary Blackbird gang

12. BUSTER, a male robin

13. GRIS, a rough city-hardened pigeon

14. HONEYBUNCH, a pigeon lady friend of GRIS'

15. VIC, a crested pigeon friend of GRIS' from Australia

16. DUCE, goblin leader of the Barbary Blackbirds

17. ROSA, gnome owner of an Italian bakery

18. OLD WOMAN, human dime store shopper

19. PHIL, gnome father of B.C.

20. CHARLIE, gnome police officer

21. NICK, gnome police officer

22. SALLY, gnome owner of SALLY'S place

23. RICKY, SALLY'S gnome bartender

24. LOLA, pixie singer at Sally's place.

25. IVY, gnome girlfriend of TOBY

26. MITCH MCCANN, gnome police lieutenant on special assignment from Daly City

27. JOHNNY, gnome police officer

28. LUKE, gnome police officer

29. MR. CHENG, Chinese gnome, father of PERRY, YI MIN and ARTHUR

30. PERRY, Chinese gnome, son of MR. CHENG

31. ARTHUR, Chinese gnome, son of MR. CHENG

32. YI MIN, Chinese gnome, daughter of MR. CHENG

33. PYXIS, leader of the pixie clan

34. IRIS, first pixie sister

35. PETALS, second pixie sister

36. DAUGHTER, gnome daughter of the OLD MAN

37. OLD MAN, gnome customer at Sally's

38. ANTHONY, ancient dragon

EXTRAS

GNOME COPS

HUMAN COPS

GNOMES ON THE STREETS

HUMANS ON THE STREETS

LADY BIRDS

GNOMES UNDERGROUND

GNOME HOTEL STAFF AND SECURITY GUARDS

HUMAN HOTEL STAFF

HUMAN HOTEL GUESTS

GNOME HOTEL GUESTS

PIXIES IN THE PIXIE CAMP

GNOME CHILDREN

HUMAN CHILDREN

SALLY'S MULTIETHNIC GNOME BAND

SALLY'S GNOME PATRONS

SALLY'S GNOME BODY GUARDS

HUMAN CROOKS AT HOTEL

SALLY'S GNOME WAITRESSES

HUMAN DIME STORE SHOPPERS

GOBLINS AND TROLLS

GNOMES AT THE POKER GAME

VOICE OF HUMAN DRIVER

CHINESE GNOME SEA CAPTAIN

CHINESE GNOME SAILORS

GLASS WINDOW REPAIR GNOME

EXT. SAN FRANCISCO NEIGHBORHOOD – 1935 – NIGHT

MARLIN (V.O.)

It began on a Thursday in the middle of November. The rain came down like steely needles being shot into a haystack. The lightening lit up the sky like a bushfire, revealing the severed limbs of <u>wind-beaten Deodara</u>. . . . An outdoor chair and then a table just missed my head by a couple of inches. It was the kind of night that made you want to hide under a blanket; only my blanket was a black night sky dotted with stars you couldn't see and a chill in the air so cold you couldn't move. My name's Jack Marlin. I'm a front-lawn dick, a gnome detective. No, not like that poor guy over there chained to the birdbath; I'm the real McCoy. Some people say I'm lucky. I say, I'm just a guy trying to get through another rainy night.

DISSOLVE TO:

EXT. MARLIN'S FRONT LAWN – NEXT DAY – SUNSET

The yard reveals damage from the storm. Flashes of light from a broken street lamp give the effect of a neon sign, the kind seen flashing outside the window of a detective's office in a Hollywood movie.

MARLIN sits on a garden ledge facing the street, legs stretched out, feet crossed resting on the edge of an overturned lawn chair, arms folded behind his head, detective's fedora shading his eyes and worn over his gnome cap, which is folded over to one side like the cap of a Santa's elf.

Behind him at the base of a human house is a gnome-size office door with a glass window and gold lettering that reads JACK MARLIN, PRIVATE DETECTIVE.

MARLIN (V.O.) (CONT'D)

The next day was a Friday just after sunset. I was resting, still chilled to the bone, from an all-night surveillance . . . when she cut through the azaleas. She was the sweetest little two-foot pixie of a gnome you ever saw. She had a point on her pretty little hat so sharp it could put your eye out. I could see myself playing Valentino to her Lady Diana. She said her name was Buttercup and that her friends called her B.C. She said I could call her B.C. and her eyes twinkled, or maybe it was just a reflection from the broken street lamp.

EXT. FLASHBACK – BACKYARD OF DESERTED HOUSE – DAY

B.C. talks to MARLIN without audio. Her lips are moving and MARLIN is listening. The shadowy scene reveals B.C. peering through a loose board in her backyard fence, observing a suspicious looking group of gnomes huddled together in the adjacent yard.

BACK TO SCENE:

EXT. MARLIN'S FRONT LAWN – NEXT DAY – SUNSET

MARLIN (V.O.) (CONT'D)

But when she explained the reason for her visit, I knew she was up to her pretty little point in trouble – the kind of trouble that smelled of blackmail, murder, and revenge.

BUTTERCUP (B.C.)

They say you got connections underground.

MARLIN (V.O.)

I told her I had a few. I wondered who had sent her and what her angle was. She had an almost sad, faraway look like she'd been looking for someone or something all her life.

(beat)

Up here on the surface, on most days, everything seems peaceful, the promise of serenity. But underneath this placid green roof is the dripping, crystalline, cavernous world where a different set of rules apply – a seedy, rooty underworld where deals are made and things kept hidden. . . . I asked myself whether I was ready to go underground again, ready to take the gamble, and maybe this time, stay underground permanently.

BEGIN TITLES

Jazz music reminiscent of John Cameron's Philip Marlowe score.

GNOME NOTES: Real gnomes are perfectly proportioned humanoids though they are just over two feet tall. They are of all nationalities and invisible to humans.

The male gnomes do not have long beards or boots, nor do they wear dunce-like caps. Their caps are made of soft material like those of Santa's elves and are usually folded over to one side. Over these, gnomes wear hats that signify their profession such as a police cap or fedora.

Female gnomes wear a smaller version of the gnome cap which is arranged on their heads in a variety of ways with points of various heights and frequently accessorized with veils, feathers, flowers or fruit, thus giving them a stylish, even outrageous 1930's look.

The two primary features that distinguish gnomes from humans are their size and their gnome hats. Apart from these characteristics, gnomes look and act exactly like the humans walking the streets of San Francisco during the 1930s.

The San Francisco gnomes have found it convenient to live within the infrastructure of the human city; however, they have made certain modifications to buildings in order to access hotel elevators, restaurants, stores and other places of business.

Preferring to use mainly human transportation, they climb unseen inside taxicabs and police cars, jump on automobile running boards, and ride on ferryboats, trolleys and cable cars.

The uncanny thing about gnomes is that they have the ability, by virtue of their will, to interact with any human-made object and still remain invisible, whereas humans cannot interact with gnome-made objects. For instance, a human would pass right through a gnome or gnome-made object while walking down the street. Gnomes, on the other hand, can carry and sometimes conceal a small human-made object by putting it in their pockets or under their clothing.

The gnomes' special abilities also apply to goblins and trolls both of whom have humanoid form and wear 1930's gangster-style clothing. These creatures generally avoid gnomes and humans altogether except for those times when they conspire to get gnomes to do their dirty work, thus giving some gnomes a bad name.

The animal characters talk and to the audience look bigger than life because they are being seen through the eyes of the gnomes.

INT. MARLIN'S OFFICE – MONDAY MORNING

After the beginning titles, the scene opens with MARLIN sitting at his desk on Monday morning. From here there are a series of four flashbacks as he recalls his investigation of B.C.'S story over the weekend. The series concludes with B.C. arriving at MARLIN'S office.

The flashbacks in order: 1. a visit to CHIEF PARKS, 2. visits to MARLIN'S animal contacts in the City and their stories, 3. remembering his association with B.C.'S father, and 4. going over the details of B.C.'S story while walking along the street on his way to her house and his subsequent investigation of the scene she described.

MARLIN (V.O.) (CONT'D)

On Monday morning, I was sitting at my desk waiting for B.C. to return. I'd made a few calls over the weekend. What B.C. told me about the gnomes on the other side of the fence was true. And I'd paid a friendly visit to a no-non-sense chief of gnome police.

INT. FLASHBACK – GNOME POLICE STATION / PARKS' OFFICE – DAY

SFX: Phones ringing / clicking of typewriter keys

PARKS

(with a deep voice and slight Irish accent)

Jackie Marlin. What brings you to this side of town?

MARLIN (V.O.)

I didn't want to mention B.C., not until I knew more about what was going on. So I decided to act casual.

MARLIN

So I hear there's been some trouble in town?

PARKS

Cut the chatter Marlin. You forget who you're talking to. We've got a citywide problem here. . . .

While PARKS is speaking, the scene reveals shadowy images of criminal chaos. Gnome figures can be seen running down back alleys being chased by gnome cops, jumping onto the running boards of human getaway cars and suspiciously moving around the City in gangs.

MARLIN (V.O.)

Parks proceeded to tell me about an anonymous group of renegade gnomes terrorizing the City and whose numbers were steadily increasing. Yet apart from their use of the City's infrastructure and transportation, gnomes are forbidden to interfere with humans. And in spite of the fact that they're invisible, Parks was not about to tolerate any who crossed the line and meddled in human affairs.

PARKS

But worst of all, I've had a few reports that some of these guys have been seen meeting in back alleys and out-of-the way places with creatures from the underground.

MARLIN

Anything I can do?

PARKS

Now that you're here Jackie, we can use your help. We want to track these guys down and find out what they're up to. We suspect they're mostly local, but no one's been able to

PARKS (CONT'D)

identify them. An old knothole peeper like you ought to be able to scrounge up a few clues.

MARLIN

Sure. I'll stay in touch.

CUT TO:

EXT. CITY STREET / PARK – DAY

MARLIN crosses the street. His jacket pockets are bulging with small brown paper bags and he is holding a package wrapped in butcher paper. He steps up onto the curb and enters a small city park.

MARLIN (V.O.)

I left the precinct with no more information than when I began. I had a few contacts in the City, but my first stop was a pet supply on the west end of Market. My pockets bulging with nuts, seeds, a can of anchovies, and a large soup bone, I proceeded with caution to make my first contact. Standing at the foot of an old oak on the grounds of a well-kept city park, I began to tap on the trunk with my house key.

Unexpectedly, a squirrel quickly runs up from behind MARLIN, climbs over his shoulder, and jumps down in front of him. He has already been in one of his pockets and is eating a nut.

SHERWOOD

Got ya Marlin.

MARLIN

Hey Sherry, how's the family?

SHERWOOD

We're doin' okay Jackie. What can I do for you?

MARLIN

I need the dope on some action.

SHERWOOD

You're not talkin' to a blind man. There's plenty goin' on this side of the City. . . .

SHERWOOD speaks to MARLIN without audio. The scene reveals shadowy gnome figures engaged in criminal activities similar to the ones described by PARKS.

MARLIN (V.O.)

Sherry confirmed Chief Parks' information on back-alley meetings. He described a few local robberies and said he had observed an increase in petty crimes among some of the younger gnomes in his area. I thanked him for his help and handed him a little burlap sack filled with nuts.

MARLIN

A little something for the family.

MARLIN (V.O.)

He responded with a gracious bow. Then with a twinkle in his eye and a snap of this tail he was gone in a flash.

(beat)

My next stop was the south side. I caught a trolley and headed for Claudine's.

CUT TO:

EXT. END OF A CUL DE SAC – CLAUDINE'S PORCH – DAY

CLAUDINE is a svelte, but somewhat aged, calico alley cat. She is sunning herself on the front porch of a little house at the end of a cul de sac. Sitting next to her is a little brown pug dog also taking in the sun. MARLIN approaches and they both look up.

CLAUDINE

Hey Marlin! How are ya? I was just sayin' to little Chester here, where's Marlin these days?

CHESTER runs over to MARLIN wagging his tail.

MARLIN

Hi Claudine. Chester.

CHESTER

(enthusiastically)

Marlin! You got a job for us?

CLAUDINE

Hey Ches, don't volunteer me. We haven't heard the details yet.

MARLIN

Just some info.

CLAUDINE

Okay shoot big boy, what do you want to know?

MARLIN

I've been hearin' stories about a group of renegade gnomes and connections with the underground. Know anything about it?

CHESTER

Plenty! Claudie and I were –

CLAUDINE

Hey, I wanted to tell it Ches. Ah, go ahead.

(to Marlin)

How can you resist that little face? Huh Marlin?

CHESTER

Claudie and I were out for a walk the other night when we saw a whole group of gnomes coming towards us. . . .

CUT TO:

EXT. FLASHBACK – CITY STREET – LATE NIGHT

CLAUDINE

Quick Ches, let's hide in here.

CHESTER and CLAUDINE hide in the bushes and overhear the gnomes' conversation as they walk past them in single file. They are discussing how they robbed the City Mint. The faces of the gnomes are shadowy but the voices are those of AARON, RUFE, DANNY, JASE, and TOBY.

AARON

What did you get Rufe?

RUFE

(looking over his shoulder)

I got about fifty cents. How about you Aaron?

AARON

It's too embarrassing to say.

RUFE

(looking straight ahead again)

What did you get Danny?

DANNY

I got a dime. Hey Jase, what did you get?

JASE

(voice fading in the distance)

I got about a dollar in nickels. What did you get Toby?

TOBY

(angry whisper fading)

I got a whole lotta nothin'.

AARON

(under his breath)

This Mint job wasn't such a good idea.

BACK TO SCENE

EXT. CLAUDINE'S PORCH – DAY

CHESTER

(to Marlin)

Yeah, like they were gonna knock over Fort Knox. They'd broken into the place and tripped an alarm. I guess they barely had time to stick a few coins in their pockets before Parks' boys arrived.

MARLIN gives them the anchovies and soup bone.

CLAUDINE

Say Marlin, I've always said you're an okay guy. Yeah, I was jus telling little Chester here, you always play fair.

CHESTER

Thanks Marlin.

(extending his paw)

If you ever need anything just give us a call.

CLAUDINE

(to Chester)

That's right Ches.

(to Marlin)

We'll see ya around Marlin.

MARLIN (V.O.)

I hoped for their sakes I didn't have to take them up on their offer.

CUT TO:

EXT. CITY STREET / PARK – DAY

MARLIN arrives at another small city park.

MARLIN (V.O.) (CONT'D)

I decided to get a bird's eye view of things and went over to Buster's place on the east side. Buster was one of those health nuts, always exercising and worried about growing old. His exercises took him high up over the City where he got a good look at things and would <u>share</u> that view for a price. I found Buster out on a limb surrounded by a group of chirpy dames and I called up to him.

BUSTER is a robin redbreast.

MARLIN

How much do you want for a song?

BUSTER

(with a smile of recognition)

In what key man?

(to the lady birds)

Excuse me ladies, duty calls.

BUSTER flies down to a lower branch where MARLIN is standing and they face one another.

BUSTER (CONT'D)

Marlin, Marlin, Marlin. You're lookin' good for a guy who spends his time snoopin' around in other people's affairs. Well Shamus my man, I know just what kinda song you're lookin' for.

MARLIN (V.O.)

I felt like lighting up a cigarette, but I knew I'd get flack from Buster, so I reached in my pocket for a stick match.

BUSTER

I've never seen anything like it. The whole east side of the City's gone crazy. Gnomes stealing from humans, gnomes stealing from gnomes, and in the broad daylight! It just ain't right Marlin. It's unhealthy you know?

MARLIN (V.O.) (CONT'D)

I left Buster with a bag of seed and proceeded towards the Mission District to meet a character very unlike Buster.

CUT TO:

EXT. OUTSIDE A MOM-AND-POP GROCERY STORE – DAY

MARLIN sees GRIS sitting on the curb in front of a grocery store. He is a rough, city-hardened pigeon.

MARLIN

Is that you Gris?

GRIS

Hey, I was expecting you Marlin.

MARLIN

How'd you know I was in this part of town?

GRIS

A little lady bird told me. Does Buster think just because he's strong and handsome, he's the only one who can get the girls?

MARLIN

If that was the case, it wouldn't leave much hope for the rest of us.

GRIS

You got a great sense of humor Marlin. I hear you're lookin' for information about some gnomes and some guys from the underground?

MARLIN

I don't think I mentioned the underground to Buster.

GRIS

That's right, you didn't but I got other sources. When Marlin's out snoopin' for information it pays to get some. You know what I mean? Anyway, I like you Marlin. I'd give it to you for nothin'. And besides, you and me, we got to keep this city together.

While GRIS is talking a lady pigeon named HONEYBUNCH flies down and cuddles up to him. She is one of the same birds who had been keeping company with BUSTER.

GRIS (CONT'D)

You see that gnome bakery?

Located at the base of a human bakery is a small awning and the entrance to an Italian gnome bakery called Rosa's.

MARLIN

Yeah. Rosa's place.

GRIS

Last week a couple of gnomes tried to rob it. I couldn't believe my eyes. They were the daffiest pair I ever saw. . . .

CUT TO:

EXT. FLASHBACK – OUTSIDE A MOM-AND-POP GROCERY STORE – DAY

GRIS and his friend VIC, a crested pigeon from Australia, are drinking beer and eating chips in front of the mom-and-pop grocery where GRIS hangs out. About half a block away at the end of a nearby alley The DUCE is giving instructions to DANNY and AARON.

The DUCE is a good-looking, but foul-tempered gnome. He is tall, wears a beige wide-brimmed fedora over his gnome cap, stylish suit, and highly polished wingtip shoes.

CUT TO:

EXT. ALLEYWAY – DAY

DUCE

(to Danny and Aaron)

You two head over to that bakery and bring me back some dough.

DANNY

(trying to act tough)

Do you want us to rough up the lady or what?

DUCE

Just go in and get the money. I'll meet you back here when you've done the job.

AARON

But what –

DUCE

No excuses. Just get the money.

AARON

Okay Duce. Sure we can do it.

DUCE leaves.

DANNY

(to Aaron)

What are you tryin' to do make us look like sissies or something?

AARON

Let's get this over with. This isn't exactly the kinda thing I had in mind when I became a Blackbird.

INT. MEMORY FLASHBACK – INSIDE THE MINE – NIGHT

AARON momentarily recalls the Barbary Blackbird initiation ceremony. Dream-like scenes show AARON, DANNY, RUFE, TOBY, and JASE standing in a line of renegade gnome recruits receiving their Blackbird armbands. Smoky flames leap up from a brazier and eerie shadows dance on a jagged cave wall. The armbands are red, black and beige with the image of a Barbary blackbird on them.

BACK TO SCENE

EXT. ALLEYWAY – DAY

AARON comes back to himself. He and DANNY turn to look after DUCE but they are surprised to see that he has mysteriously disappeared from their sight. They exit the alley and enter the bakery oblivious to the fact that they are being observed by GRIS and VIC.

INT. ROSA'S ITALIAN BAKERY – DAY

ROSA is a beautiful Sophia Loren-like Italian gnome with a fiery temper. Instead of a gnome cap she wears a scarf that resembles one.

ROSA

(in a sweet tone of voice in English with
an Italian accent)

Hot rolls. We have hot rolls today. Just out of the oven.

DANNY and AARON approach the counter enticed by the sights and smells of the bakery.

ROSA (CONT'D)

What can I get for you gentlemen?

AARON

(seeming to lose his nerve)

Uh, I would like a loaf of that sourdough bread, a half dozen hot rolls and one of those cakes.

ROSA places AARON'S bag on the counter. He picks it up and ROSA turns to DANNY.

ROSA

And you sir?

DANNY looks at AARON who is standing beside him holding a large brown paper shopping bag with a long loaf of bread sticking out of the top and decides to go along with the flow.

DANNY

I'll have a dozen breadsticks, six cookies, a panettone,

(pointing)

and uh . . . a couple of those rolls.

ROSA puts DANNY'S bag on the counter. DANNY picks up his bag while ROSA turns her back to add up their purchases on a large brass cash register. The two gnomes glance at one another as if to say, "What do we do now?"

ROSA

(to Danny)

That'll be $2.50 for you and

(to Aaron)

and $2.00 for you.

ROSA turns away from the two gnomes and opens the till. AARON takes one of DANNY'S bread sticks and puts it in his jacket pocket like a gun.

AARON

(in a shaky voice)

W-We'll also take the money in your drawer.

ROSA quickly turns back to face them and sees the supposed gun muzzle pointing at her. She suddenly lunges from around the counter and grabs the loaf of French bread sticking out of the top of AARON'S bag and furiously beats both gnomes over the head and shoulders.

Still holding their bags, the gnomes run for the exit. All the while ROSA is yelling at them in Italian, running after them and beating them with the loaf of bread.

ROSA

(furiously in a Neapolitan Italian dialect
subtitled in English)

Do you think my mama and papa worked all their lives so you can come here and rob us? I'll kill you! I'll kill you! Don't run away from me. Come back here you idiots, I want to kill you. How dare you run away? You cowards! Come back.

EXT. ROSA'S ITALIAN BAKERY – DAY

ROSA now stands on the sidewalk in front of the bakery flaying her arms, biting her hand and addressing anyone who might be listening or passing by.

ROSA (CONT'D)

(in English)

Look how brave they are! Run away you cowards! Run away!

EXT. OUTSIDE THE MOM-AND-POP GROCERY STORE – DAY

GRIS and VIC observe DANNY and AARON as they fly down the street in their direction still holding the bags.

GRIS

Unbelievable, simply unbelievable.

The gnomes run right past GRIS and VIC leaving a trail of pastry and rolls behind them.

GRIS (CONT'D)

What'd ya call that?

VIC

(with a strong Australian accent)

I'd call it pretty sloppy work.

(passing the chips to Gris)

This is better than goin' to the pictures. These wallies wouldn't last two minutes where I come from.

BACK TO SCENE

GRIS

(to Marlin)

I wouldn't be surprised if these guys were working with the undergrounds.

Couldn't be sure though, cuz I've never seen any my-self, but I got the feeling they were being put up to it. They disappeared up that alley and didn't come out for a while.

CUT TO:

EXT. FLASHBACK – ALLEYWAY – DAY

DANNY and AARON come panting back up the garage-lined alleyway, looking over their shoulders to see if anyone is behind them. In backyards on either side of the alley, high overhead, white sheets and towels pinned to pulley-driven clotheslines snap and flutter in the wind.

AARON

Whew! I thought she was following us.

DANNY

No, we're okay.

As the gnomes turn around and face the end of the alley, DUCE steps menacingly out of the shadows and with one hand simultaneously slaps them both across the face.

DUCE

You idiots! What are you trying to do?

DANNY

(apologetically to Duce)

The stuff looked so good and we were sorta hungry.

DUCE

I feed yas don't I? Aren't we a family? Okay, I'll forgive ya this time but no more slipups cuz the rest of the group might not like it.

DANNY

Okay Duce, we'll do better next . . .

Before the words are even out of DANNY'S mouth, DUCE mysteriously disappears again.

> **AARON**
>
> (startled)

Where did he go? How does he do that?

> **DANNY**

I don't know, but it gives me the creeps. Let's go find Jase and Rufe.

> **AARON**

What do you think he's making those guys do?

> **DANNY**

Anything but Rosa's I hope. If we got caught we might've gone to jail.

> **AARON**

Somehow I don't think The Duce would've cared very much about that.

DANNY does not respond but looks at AARON with an expression of concern.

BACK TO SCENE

EXT. OUTSIDE THE MOM-AND-POP GROCERY STORE – DAY

GRIS

(to Marlin)

Yep, I bet they left a trail of telltale crumbs all the way back to their hideout. They just didn't fit the criminal profile.

MARLIN

You'd make a great P.I. Gris.

MARLIN gives GRIS a bag of seed. GRIS hands the seed to his lady pigeon friend.

GRIS

(addressing the lady)

Here Honeybunch, help yourself. See ya around Marlin.

MARLIN

Take care Gris.

EXT. CITY STREET – DAY

MARLIN walks along the street.

MARLIN (V.O.)

Gris was my last stop. B.C.'S suspicions had added up right. And I had no doubt about underground connections. I headed in the direction of B.C.'s and went over the details

MARLIN (V.O.) (CONT'D)

of her story, especially a conversation she overheard on the
other side of her backyard fence.

CUT TO:

EXT. MEMORY FLASHBACK – BACKYARD OF DESERTED HOUSE –
DAY

JASE

What's the plan?

TOBY

The Duce wants us to meet him tonight, all of us. He ain't
gonna be happy about that dime-store job.

DANNY

(to Jase and Rufe)

You never told us what happened.

RUFE remains silent, but JASE pulls a long piece of wild grass out of the
ground and chews on it as he speaks.

JASE

The Duce told us to meet him in the Park. . . .

CUT TO:

EXT. FLASHBACK – CITY PARK – DAY

While The DUCE is speaking to RUFE and JASE, there is a shot of SHERRY spying on them by peeking with one beady little eye from around a tree.

DUCE

You two go over to that human establishment and do some shopping. But ya don't bring any money with yas. See?

JASE

Okay . . . but the humans can't see us anyway. So do you want us to rob the place?

DUCE

Yeah.

RUFE

What shall we take?

DUCE

As much as you can carry.

JASE and RUFE look at one another with puzzled expressions. By the time they look back, DUCE has mysteriously disappeared. The two gnomes look suspiciously around and cross the street.

INT. FIVE-AND-DIME STORE – DAY

JASE AND RUFE enter the human five-and-dime and walk down an aisle where an OLD WOMAN is examining spools of thread.

RUFE

Find something small.

JASE

But The Duce said to pick up as much as we can carry.

RUFE

Hey, what's that?

The OLD WOMAN drops a spool of thread and it rolls on the floor towards JASE. He looks down and then looks in the direction of where the spool came from. It appears as if the OLD WOMAN is staring straight at him.

JASE panics and turns to run away from the OLD WOMAN who approaches them with her cane in order to retrieve the thread. In their haste the two gnomes bump into various trays and displays of sewing notions spilling them onto the floor.

They scramble into the fabric section and peer out at their surroundings partly concealed by swaths of material.

JASE

(whispering)

That old woman saw us.

RUFE

That's impossible. We can't leave without taking something.

JASE

Okay. Okay.

JASE pockets spools of thread and thimbles that have fallen onto the floor.

RUFE

(as he picks up packages of buttons and
trim)

I feel so stupid.

JASE

Here she comes again.

The OLD WOMAN again moves in the direction of the two gnomes and reaches out for a thimble JASE is holding. To the OLD WOMAN the thimble looks as if it is floating in midair. JASE panics and alarms RUFE.

JASE and RUFE both tear down the isle knocking over more displays. Amid the growing confusion caused by the items, which look to the humans as if they are just cascading onto the floor by themselves, even RUFE begins to wonder if they are being seen.

EXT. FIVE-AND-DIME STORE – DAY

They fly out the door of the five-and-dime, their pockets full of sewing notions. JASE has a cloth measuring tape wrapped abound his ankle and is trailing it across the street as they head back to the park.

EXT. CITY PARK – DAY

JASE (CONT'D)

Where's The Duce?

RUFE

He probably cut out on us.

DUCE is nowhere to be seen. Meanwhile, the human police arrive at the five-and-dime, sirens blaring. There is another shot of SHERRY still peering at the scene from behind the tree.

BACK TO SCENE

EXT. BACKYARD OF DESERTED HOUSE – DAY

> **AARON**
>
> (to Jase)

So how much loot did you get?

> **DANNY**
>
> (jokingly)

A piece of tailor's chalk and a knitting needle?

> **JASE**
>
> (to Danny)

That's not funny. I still think that old lady saw us.

> **RUFE**

The human coppers were goin' crazy trying to figure out what happened.

> **AARON**

Maybe that's what The Duce wanted?

> **TOBY**
>
> (to Aaron angrily)

What'd ya mean by that?

> **RUFE**
>
> (to Toby)

He didn't mean nothin'.

TOBY

I'm bringing in a couple of new guys. They want to join the group and The Duce says we're goin' underground.

BACK TO SCENE

EXT. CITY STREET – DAY

MARLIN continues to walk along the street on his way to B.C.'S house and now recalls his friendship with her father.

MARLIN (V.O.)

As I continued on my way to B.C.'s remembering the details of her story and the gnomes' conversation, I also recalled my friendship with her father.

(beat)

I hadn't only checked on B.C.'S story, I checked on B.C.. Miss Buttercup was from the other side of the neighborhood. Not in the way one might think. She had real class. Turns out I knew her father. He had class too. Her old man and I went way back. I remembered a night at Sally's Place about ten years ago. . . .

INT. MEMORY FLASHBACK – TEN YEARS AGO – SALLY'S – NIGHT

SFX: Clack of poker chips and shuffling of cards

MARLIN and B.C.'S father are playing a friendly game of poker with a group of other gnomes.

PHIL

Say Jackie, remember the time we cracked that case no one could figure? We trailed 'em all the way to the underground.

MARLIN

You're the best Phil. Those were the days.

BACK TO SCENE

MARLIN arrives at B.C.'S house.

EXT. B.C.'S YARD – DAY

MARLIN (V.O.)

When I arrived at B.C.'s., a little Victorian style cottage, no one was home, but everything was just as she had described – the loose board in the fence, the vacant house next door,

(looks through hole in fence)

and the foot prints in the dirt where the gnomes had been standing. I looked down at my feet and saw a broken twig.

(picks up the twig)

Then somehow I knew B.C. had been seen. As she moved away from the fence, she must have inadvertently stepped on the twig unaware that she had alerted Rufe to her presence. From there I could only imagine . . . and in my mind I heard the tail end of a conversation that B.C. never heard – a conversation we'd all live to regret.

MARLIN'S P.O.V. – He imagines the gnomes' reaction when discovering B.C.'s presence.

RUFE motions to the others to be quiet and directs their attention to the hole in the fence.

RUFE

It's that copper's daughter.

TOBY

Shut her up. Any way you have to. I'll tell The Duce we got a problem.

BACK TO SCENE

EXT. B.C.'S YARD – DAY

MARLIN (V.O.) (CONT'D)

B.C. had given me a pretty clear description of the five faces on the other side of the fence – faces that began to dog me like a bad penny.

MARLIN'S P.O.V. – He bends down and looks through the hole in the fence a second time.

MARLIN (V.O.) (CONT'D)

They shadowed my every footstep and haunted my waking dreams.

MEMORY FLASHBACK

While being described by MARLIN, RUFE, JASE, DANNY, AARON, and TOBY are idly standing around the lot trying to act cool, backslapping, shoving, elbowing, and kicking up patches of dead grass and junk on the ground.

MARLIN (V.O.) (CONT'D)

Rufe was a big guy with two people inside. One was a gentleman and the other a friend of The Duce. Eventually he'd have to make a choice and I wondered which one of himself would win out in the end.

(beat)

The youngest member of the bunch was Jase, just a simple city kid from a broken family. The Duce had promised to make him a Blackbird and the kid was ready to sell his soul for a pair of wings.

(beat)

Danny was tall for a gnome, olive skinned and brown eyed. He reminded me of the cowardly lion from The Wizard of Oz, only he wasn't too afraid to resist the temptations of The Duce. Aaron was freckled and wore glasses. He was a dead ringer for a criminal lawyer I once knew except he wasn't spending his time defending the innocent. He was playin' from a marked deck on the wrong side of the law.

(beat)

And then there was Toby, the pretty one. . . .

BACK TO SCENE

EXT. MARLIN'S OFFICE – MONDAY MORNING

MARLIN (V.O.)

Yep, the weekend had paid off alright and now I had enough dope to begin fitting the pieces together. I returned home Sunday night—a nice little bungalow affair nestled at the base of a human house. It afforded me an office with a glass window that read JACK MARLIN, PRIVATE DETECTIVE in gold lettering and a spacious front yard complete with birdbath and ceramic gnome. That same Monday I was leaning back in my chair, feet on desk, cup of coffee in hand, when B.C. crossed the front yard and entered my office.

B.C.

Good Morning.

MARLIN

(pulling out a chair for her)

Please, have a seat.

B.C.

Thank you.

MARLIN

(seating himself again)

Why didn't you tell me who your father was?

B.C.

Just careful I guess. I wasn't sure –

MARLIN

Whose side I was on?

B.C.

Something like that.

MARLIN

Why did you come to me?

B.C.

My dad told me if I ever needed anything –

MARLIN

Yeah, I know.

MARLIN (V.O.)

I usually charged $30 a day for my services plus expenses, but Phil had been a good friend. Things weren't the same after he died. Now here was his daughter all grown up and asking me for help.

MARLIN

Ok B.C., I'll see what I can do. I think you take after your old man. Do you play poker?

B.C.

Sure. Why do you ask?

MARLIN

Just curious. It matters to you . . . about things. . . .

B.C. does not answer, but gives MARLIN a perceptive smile and leaves.

MARLIN (V.O.)

She was Phil's daughter alright. She had the same beautiful smile. The kinda smile that made you believe in yourself. I grabbed my hat and coat and intended to follow her home, but no sooner had she left my property when trouble climbed over the hedge.

DUCE

Listen Marlin, we've been watching you.

MARLIN

Yeah, see anything interesting?

DUCE

Yeah, we seen you gettin' real nosey lawn dick. You've been talking to that copper's daughter.

MARLIN

Maybe you'll tell me what business that is of yours?

DUCE

Everything that happens is our business. Stay in your own yard and you won't get hurt.

MARLIN

I never did like being bossed by a bully.

DUCE

In that case I'm comin' back Marlin, and I'm not comin' alone. You'd better back off sapshoe if you know what's good for you. They call me The Duce. And I don't want ya to forget it.

MARLIN

You seem like more of a dupe to me.

DUCE

I don't like you Marlin. But I wanna give ya a little something to remember me by.

DUCE punches MARLIN in the jaw and almost knocks him off his feet. MARLIN returns the favor and knocks DUCE into the street. DUCE gets up quickly and disappears.

MARLIN (V.O.)

Before I could grab him and make him talk, he disappeared, and I mean literally disappeared. Only he left me a calling card, a presence that made my skin crawl.

EXT. CITY STREET – DAY

MARLIN sets out on foot for B.C.'S.

MARLIN (V.O.) (CONT'D)

I knew I had to get to B.C., fast. I hoped she had sense enough to lie low. I had just turned the corner of B.C.'s block when I felt an iron grip on my wrist and my arm being wrenched up behind my back.

RUFE and TOBY attack MARLIN, put a sack over his head, and shove him into the back of human taxi that happens to be waiting nearby.

RUFE

You were warned you lousy, no good do gooder.

EXT. LOMBARD STREET – DAY

The taxi makes a stop at the top of Lombard Street (the crookedest street in the world) where AARON, DANNY, and JASE are waiting. MARLIN is dragged out of the car and forced into a wooden barrel. The lid is secured and the barrel is pushed over the hill.

The barrel crashes from side-to-side all the way down the street. When it reaches the bottom, it breaks open and Marlin comes sprawling out.

CUT TO:

INT. GNOME POLICE STATION / PARKS' OFFICE – AFTERNOON

SFX: Phones ringing / clicking of typewriter keys

MARLIN (V.O.)

I staggered back to Parks' office seeing double.

PARKS

I can see you've been out making friends again Jackie. Who are your new pals?

MARLIN

A mug named Duce for one.

PARKS

Never heard of him. Can you describe him?

MARLIN

Yeah, pretty as a picture. But if you ask me, I think there's somethin' foul, hairy, and hateful goin' on under all that charm.

PARKS

Sounds like a case for you and Phil.

MARLIN

Yeah, we made a good team.

PARKS

Is this Duce a client of yours?

MARLIN

Nah, just a troublemaker.

PARKS

Did you get a description of your other buddies?

MARLIN

No.

(short laugh at the joke with obvious pain)

I couldn't see their faces, but just as I was being forced into the taxi, I noticed one of them had an armband with a blackbird.

PARKS

I'll stake out the neighborhood. Meanwhile, go home and lie down. You look terrible.

EXT. OUTSIDE THE POLICE STATION – AFTERNOON

MARLIN, CHARLIE and NICK climb into the back of a human police car headed in the direction of B.C.'S house.

MARLIN (V.O.)

Parks sent a couple of his boys to escort me home, but I convinced them to go with me to B.C.'s. I figured B.C.'s place was being watched and I needed someone to watch my back while I got her out. Thank heaven, Parks' boys were familiar with my tactics and didn't ask too many questions.

The police car makes a stop across the street from B.C.'s and MARLIN exits. The two human cops in the front seat are trying to make out a fuzzy message on the police radio and do not notice that the back door of the car has quietly opened and closed again.

MARLIN

(waving to Charlie and Nick)

Thanks fellahs.

CHARLIE and NICK keep an eye on MARLIN as he crosses the street. Still shaken from the barrel ride, MARLIN holds his stomach as he walks.

MARLIN (V.O.)

Apparently B.C. had taken the precaution of staying with friends and had just come home the moment I arrived. I told her to pack a bag. Then we hopped a trolley headed in the direction of the Presidio. I was going to take her to a little place I knew across the water.

SFX: Snaps of electricity and sparks from the trolley's overhead power lines

CUT TO:

EXT. PRESIDIO – FERRY – EVENING

MARLIN and B.C. take the ferry across the Golden Gate Strait. During the crossing, MARLIN observes the Golden Gate Bridge as it looked under construction in 1935.

MARLIN (V.O.) (CONT'D)

On most nights, the trip across the Strait was a pleasant one. The fog rolling in off the bay, the city lights, they kept a guy's thoughts off himself. But tonight the fog clawed at me with ominous tentacles. The phantom towers and tangle of wire from the construction of the bridge left me feeling –

B.C.

(looking back towards the city)

It's beautiful, isn't it, the water and the lights?

MARLIN

(still looking in the direction of the bridge)

Yeah.

EXT. OUTSIDE MUIR WOODS – NIGHT

MARLIN (V.O.)

From the ferry landing, it was a short walk to the gravity train that takes passengers down into Muir Woods.

EXT. ON THE GRAVITY TRAIN – NIGHT

MARLIN (V.O.) (CONT'D)

Our destination was Sally's place, the best little nectar joint this side of Heaven. I knew Sally would look after Miss Buttercup while I figured out my next move.

CUT TO:

INT. SALLY'S PLACE – NIGHT

MARLIN and B.C. enter Sally's place. He takes off his fedora and trench coat and hangs them on a stand in the corner. Although Sally's place is located on the edge of the woods, it has a lounge-like atmosphere. The room is slightly smoky and the décor homey.

SALLY

Hey Marlin where've you been?

MARLIN

(hugging her)

Good to see ya Sally. Sally, this is Buttercup.

SALLY looks at B.C. and B.C. extends her hand. They are instant friends.

B.C.

(to Sally)

Call me B.C.

SALLY

It's been too long Marlin. Something tells me B.C.'s not your girlfriend.

MARLIN

Nope. I need to keep her under wraps for a while.

SALLY

Sure. I got a nice room for her.

(to B.C.)

C'mon honey, I'll show you where to put your things.

MARLIN seats himself at the bar and is greeted by Ricky the bartender.

RICKY

(pours Marlin a drink)

How ya been Jackie?

MARLIN

Not too bad. How are things around here?

RICKY

Quiet. But you know Sally. She runs a tight ship. She won't put up with any nonsense in her neck of the woods.

SALLY and B.C. emerge from a side door. SALLY seats B.C. at a table in the corner and approaches the bar.

SALLY

Ricky, a Silver Fizz for B.C.

(to Marlin)

They're on the house.

MARLIN

(to Ricky)

The same again.

MARLIN picks up both drinks and walks over to the table where B.C. is sitting. He hands her a drink and sits down. MARLIN and B.C.'S lips are moving, but only the 1930's music and the voice of LOLA, the pixie Jazz singer, can be heard.

MARLIN (V.O.)

We stayed the night at Sally's where B.C. and I spent most of the evening talking and listening to an angel sing.

LOLA, the pixie Jazz singer, is slim and fair-skinned with short curly blonde hair. Her voice and appearance are a tribute to Lola Albright (<u>Peter Gunn</u>). She is singing something romantic. The all-gnome band is made up of various nationalities.

CUT TO:

EXT. MARLIN'S FRONT LAWN – MORNING

MARLIN arrives home. The yard is a shambles. The ceramic gnome that was chained to the birdbath has been wrenched off and is now stuck up side down in the ground by its long pointed dunce cap.

MARLIN (V.O.) (CONT'D)

The next morning I headed back across the Bay. When I returned home I was greeted by a terrible sight. I had a few visitors the night before and they weren't the sort I'd be inviting back anytime soon. In fact, they never left. They were hiding behind the hedge waiting for me as I crossed the yard.

TOBY

Hey Mr. Moto.

MARLIN

(surveying the yard)

The name's Marlin and I don't think I hired any decorators. You mugs don't impress me as the sensitive type.

RUFE

Look Mac, we want that girl.

DANNY and JASE come out from hiding and grab MARLIN from behind. AARON pulls back an upturned fist aimed at MARLIN'S gut.

TOBY

You'd better tell us where you stowed that dame if you know what's good for ya.

MARLIN (V.O.)

I manage to escape their hold by wrenching one arm free and giving Jase a good sock on the jaw.

Jase keels over and lands in the wet grass.

MARLIN (V.O.) (CONT'D)

Surprised by this unexpected turn of events and not wanting to draw any more attention to themselves, the gnomes decide to return to their hideout. But as they depart, I notice they're all wearing Blackbird armbands.

CUT TO:

INT. GNOME HIDEOUT – DAY

The gnome's hideout is TOBY'S upscale apartment in an Art Deco building. The five gnomes arrive at the apartment and are greeted by TOBY'S girlfriend IVY. She is wearing a fashionable 1930's dress and costume jewelry.

TOBY

When we find that girl we're gonna put her eyes out for snoopin'.

IVY

(fearfully)

B.C.'S a nice girl. What do you want to hurt her for?

TOBY

Whose side are you on? Didn't I buy you those nice things with that money we got? Didn't The Duce arrange for these upscale digs?

IVY

I'm on your side Toby. I just don't want to see anybody get hurt.

TOBY slaps IVY across the face and knocks her down. RUFE starts to help her up.

TOBY

Leave her alone Rufe.

TOBY and the others leave the apartment. IVY is alone and slowly gets up off the floor. She packs a suitcase and makes a phone call.

IVY

I want to speak to Chief Parks. Yes, I'll wait.

SPLIT-SCREEN – IVY AND CHIEF PARKS ON THE PHONE – DAY

PARKS

This is Chief Parks.

IVY

I'm calling to report a robbery and a murder. Well . . . the murder hasn't happened yet.

PARKS

Can you give me more details?

IVY

Yes. His name is Toby. He was involved in that bakery job on the north side and also –

PARKS

Where is Toby now?

IVY

This afternoon he'll be at the Saint Francis Hotel. They're planning to rob the safe.

PARKS

Can you describe him?

IVY

(with tears)

He has red hair and –

PARKS

What is this murder you spoke of?

IVY

The girl, B.C. . . . . They're lookin' for her. The whole thing is run by a guy named Duce –

IVY (CONT'D)

(hears something)

That's all I can say.

(hangs up)

CUT TO:

INT. GNOME POLICE STATION / PARKS' OFFICE – DAY

SFX: Phones ringing / clicking of typewriter keys

PARKS is just coming out of his office.

PARKS

Marlin, I'm glad you're here. I just had a tip-off. I think it was the girlfriend of one of the Blackbird boys. She called to squeal on a guy named Toby. I think you know him.

MARLIN

Yeah. I know him.

MARLIN (V.O.)

Toby was as pretty as a coral snake and just as deadly. He had teeth that were just a little too white, black eyes and fiery red hair slicked back stylishly under his gnome cap. After The Duce, he was the obvious leader of the pack.

PARKS

She squealed on your friend Duce as well. I got a plan to nail 'em. Let's go.

MARLIN and PARKS go outside the police station and jump onto the running board of a human police car headed in the direction of the Saint Francis Hotel. MARLIN grips the door handle with one hand and holds his hat on with the other.

MARLIN (V.O.)

There are three things that stand in the way of committing the perfect crime — greed, boasting, and girlfriends.

(beat)

By coincidence, there were two jewelers' conventions being held at the Saint Francis Hotel, one gnome and the other human. And no doubt the hotel safe would be full of the stuff. Parks set up a sting that would get his men inside.

CUT TO:

EXT. CLAUDINE'S PORCH – DAY

CLAUDINE and HONEYBUNCH (GRIS'S lady friend) are gossiping about the news around town. CHES is lying in the sun taking it all in.

CLAUDINE

Any news about Marlin?

HONEYBUNCH

Plenty! I've got it on good authority that he's goin' in with the cops to nail them crooks when they crack the safe at the Saint Francis.

CHES looks up all eyes and ears. MARLIN is his hero and he wants to be just like him. He suddenly gets up and disappears through a pet door in his house which is across from Claudine's. After a few minutes he emerges wearing his doggie trench coat and little fedora with a tiny gnome cap underneath.

CLAUDINE

Now jus where do you think you're goin'?

CHESTER

C'mon Claudie. You know you want to go along.

HONEYBUNCH

If he ain't the craziest little dog. Ches honey, you got real spunk. Marlin is lucky to have a friend like you.

I'll see ya later Claudie. I told Gris I'd meet him for Lunch.

CLAUDINE

Tell Gris Hi from Claudie and Ches.

CHESTER does his Marlin imitation by coolly tipping his hat towards HONEYBUNCH.

CHESTER

(to Honeybunch)

See ya around angel.

CLAUDINE

(to Chester)

Alright, you win. Let's go.

EXT. CITY STREET – DAY

The pair walk down the San Francisco streets past alleyways and stores. Here and there one sees human activity, cars, legs, and kids, just enough to remind the viewer that the infrastructure is a human one. But there are also many gnomes, gnome families and shopkeepers.

CHESTER sneaks around buildings like a real detective looking in both directions and trying to keep from being seen while CLAUDINE tries to keep from laughing.

CUT TO:

EXT. OUTSIDE THE HOTEL – DAY

Meanwhile, PARKS and MARLIN secretly arrive at the hotel and are greeted by MITCH MCCANN a rugged outdoors-type gnome police lieutenant and four of Parks' men (CHARLIE, NICK, JOHNNY, and LUKE). CHARLIE and NICK are the two officers who previously escorted MARLIN to B.C.'S.

CHARLIE

Hi ya Marlin.

MARLIN

(to Charlie)

Hey Charlie.

(turning towards Nick)

Nick, how's the wife?

NICK

She's doin okay. We had a girl.

JOHNNY

How's it goin' Marlin?

LUKE

Marlin.

MARLIN

(to Johnny)

Hi ya Johnny.

(to Luke)

Luke.

PARKS

Marlin, this is Lieutenant Mitch McCann on special assignment from Daly City.

Mitch, Jackie Marlin.

MCCANN

(giving a casual salute)

Marlin.

MARLIN

McCann.

MCCANN

Marlin.

PARKS

I can see you two are a couple of chips off the old block.

(to Marlin)

McCann and his boys are going in as jewelers. We've given them a description of your feathered friends.

MCCANN speaks to MARLIN while taking off his trench coat which conceals a businessman's black suit.

MCCANN

Sounds like these Blackbird boys are all smoke and no fire.

CUT TO:

INT. HOTEL BANQUETTE ROOM – DAY

Within the Saint Francis there is a gnome hotel with gnome waiters, cooks and bellboys invisibly intermingling with the humans. RUFE, DANNY, AARON, and JASE gain access to the hotel by dressing as waiters. Once inside they pause in the doorway of the main banquet room, which is being used by the humans. They watch as a human waiter flambés a dish at one end of a long buffet table heaped with food and elaborate center pieces. Fire and smoke rise impressively.

HUMAN HOTEL GUESTS

Ooh, Ahh!

(they clap)

At either end of the table are two large ice sculptures. One of the sculptures is carved in the form of a large swan with its wings spread and the other is in the form of two dolphins leaping from the waves.

CUT TO:

EXT. OUTSIDE THE HOTEL – DAY

MCCANN

(to Parks while holding a jeweler's briefcase)

Okay Chief, let's raid the nest.

PARKS

Marlin, you'd better cross the street and stay outta sight or it'll blow our cover.

CHESTER and CLAUDINE arrive across the street from the hotel. MARLIN hesitates on the corner then starts to cross the street.

MARLIN (V.O.)

There wasn't a whole lotta difference between McCann and me. He'd been to college and earned his stripes. Only now he was on the City's payroll and could afford a better pair of shoes.

But underneath those shiny noisemakers he was just another flatfoot, a guy who made a living by reading the criminal mind and by trying to sow a little justice in an unjust world.

TOBY, who has been parked in a stolen human car a few yards from the hotel entrance, sees MARLIN seemingly come out of nowhere and begin to cross the street. He aims the car in MARLIN'S direction and motions to two gnome recruits dressed as hotel security guards to push in the clutch and step on the gas.

TOBY

Alright you two, step on it. I'm gonna put that nosey knot-hole peeper outta his misery.

CHESTER suddenly realizes MARLIN is in danger when he sees the speeding car and the hateful expression on TOBY'S face behind the wheel.

CHESTER

(running into the street)

Marlin! Watch out!

SFX: Cars screeching, horns blowing, glass shattering

Cars and trucks crash into each other in a pileup.

MARLIN jumps out of the way just in time, but CHESTER is nowhere to be seen amid the rubble, yelling and confusion.

CLAUDINE

(teary eyed, hysterical)

Ches!

HUMAN (O.S.)

I think I hit something.

CUT TO:

INT. SAINT FRANCIS HOTEL – AFTERNOON

JASE, DANNY, AARON, and RUFE are making their way to the rear of the hotel where the walk-in safe is located. As they move through the hotel, they observe the Art Deco décor and activity of gnomes and humans around them.

RUFE

Okay, remember the plan. There won't be any gnome guards. So we're supposed to wait until the human guards

RUFE (CONT'D)

open the safe and then grab some of those jewel cases before they close it again.

The four humans are actually crooks disguised as security guards.

AARON

Hey! Those aren't the same guards The Duce showed us the other day. Those jerks are gonna rob our safe!

RUFE spots MCCANN and a side view of NICK pressed up against the wall just outside the door of the walk-in safe room.

RUFE

(to Aaron)

Did you see that?

AARON

What?

RUFE

(pointing to the doorway)

Over there.

DANNY

I don't see anything.

RUFE

I think they're cops.

(looks around the room for another exit)

JASE

I don't like this.

AARON

Calm down you guys no one knows we're here.

RUFE

(pointing out the alternate exit)

Not unless someone squealed.

JASE

They must've knocked out the other guards and took the keys.

One of the human crooks is watching the door while the other three are attempting to open the safe.

HUMAN CROOK (O.S.)

I think someone's comin'.

DUAL DIALOGUE: By coincidence, both MCCANN and the HUMAN POLICE emerge and shout at the same time.

HUMAN POLICEMAN	MCCANN
Police!	Police!

JASE

We're busted.

The human crooks pull out guns and fire on their own cops.

DANNY

They got guns.

Both the human crooks and the four gnomes make their escape through an open door and are pursued by both the human and gnome cops as they head in the direction of the lobby. Bullets are fired continuously by both human and gnome police, but no one is killed.

The gnome staff and hotel guests move aside when they see DANNY, RUFE, AARON, and JASE being chased by MCCANN and his men (CHARLIE, NICK, JOHNNY, and LUKE). Sometimes the gnomes and humans seem to be running head on into each other but pass right through one another.

DANNY

I've been hit.

RUFE

(not seeing any wound)

One of theirs or ours?

DANNY

Theirs I think.

JASE

Danny, human bullets can't hurt you.   You're invisible remember?

DANNY

Oh yeah.

As DANNY moves past the place where they were standing holes from the human bullets can be seen in the wall where they passed harmlessly through him.

AARON

Funny how that works.

RUFE

Just be glad it does.

RUFE, DANNY, AARON, and JASE run through an open elevator door, push a secret button, and emerge on the 13th floor which is the invisible gnome floor in the human hotel. DANNY notices that MCCANN and his men are coming out of another elevator on the same floor.

DANNY

(breaking into a run)

C'mon! We're on the gnome floor. The humans can't see us.

JASE

If we're invisible can somebody tell me why we're still running?

DANNY

Because our cops are right behind us and their bullets don't miss.

The four gnomes enter the elevator again just before the door closes and come out in the lobby. They are just in time to see the human police wrestle and handcuff one of the human crooks.

JASE

Hey, they caught one of the humans.

AARON

We're supposed to meet Toby in the back. How are we gonna get outta here?

DANNY

Oh man, that coulda been one of us.

MCCANN and his men are running down the staircase that leads to the Lobby.

RUFE

(over his shoulder)

C'mon!

The four gnomes, MCCANN and his men, the human police, and the three remaining robbers run into the banquet room. The humans upset the banquet table and the two ice sculptures at either end slide onto the polished floor and quickly glide towards DANNY, RUFE, AARON, and JASE.

JASE and RUFE jump onto the swan which is quickly picking up speed as it rushes across the floor of the banquet room. Following close behind are DANNY and AARON each astride one of the leaping dolphins. The sculptures burst through a pair of swinging doors leading to the kitchen, sail through the pantry, and out the backdoor.

EXT. OUTSIDE THE HOTEL BACK ENTRANCE – LATE AFTERNOON

The swan ice sculpture crashes into TOBY'S gnome-driven human getaway car. JASE and RUFE jump off in the nick of time and look on in terror as the dolphin ice sculpture speeds towards them. DANNY and AARON leap off the dolphins seconds before the sculpture crashes into what remains of the swan in an explosion of ice chips.

The four gnomes scramble into the getaway car and escape. MCCANN and his men still in their jeweler's disguises run out the backdoor slipping and sliding on the ice fragments.

SFX: Police siren

MCCANN

(punching his fist into the wall)

Damn!

MCCANN'S voice can barely be heard over the noise of the human police car siren passing by in pursuit of the three human crooks that got away. As they race by, MCCANN hears the famous "calling all cars" line.

The profile of the human policeman and then the back of his head can be seen as he speaks into a 1930's car microphone.

HUMAN POLICEMAN

Calling all cars.

(fading in the distance)

Calling all cars.

CUT TO:

EXT. OUTSIDE THE FRONT OF THE HOTEL – LATE AFTERNOON

CLAUDINE frantically weaves in and out between the pileup of cars looking for CHESTER.

CLAUDINE

(frantic)

Ches? Ches?

She suddenly spots CHESTER'S little fedora now badly crumpled and flattened.

CLAUDINE (CONT'D)

(grief stricken)

Ches!

As MARLIN and CLAUDINE stand side by side looking at the fedora in an agony of disbelief, a little paw suddenly steps from around a car tire. CHESTER emerges completely unscathed except for his hat.

CHESTER

Which way did they go?

CLAUDINE

(incredibly relieved)

Oh, Ches!

MARLIN

Thanks Ches, you saved my life.

CHESTER

(putting on his badly crumpled fedora)

All in a day's work Jackie.

MARLIN

(to Chester and Claudine)

I think you two better go home now

(winking at Chester)

and keep outta trouble.

CLAUDINE

See ya later Marlin. C'mon Ches, let's go home.

EXT. CITY STREET – EVENING

MARLIN walks down a chilly San Francisco street, hands in the pockets of his trench coat, collar up, and the brim of his fedora turned down against the wind and swirling sidewalk debris. He is chewing on a matchstick in the corner of his mouth.

MARLIN (V.O.)

There was no mistake about it. Toby was the fiery-haired evil genius behind the wheel of the getaway car. Apparently not everyone in Duce's gang was as stupid as they looked. Only, intelligence alone is never the mark of success. It would only be a matter of time before someone slipped up and I planned on being there when it happened.

(jumping onto the rear of a cable car)

SFX: Cable car bell

MARLIN (V.O.) (CONT'D)

I headed for Chinatown before going back to Sally's. I had an appointment to keep with an exquisitely prepared Peking duck and Charles Cheng, a longtime friend and first generation Chinese American. Cheng and his family knew more about the City than the city planners themselves.

EXT. ENTRANCE TO CHINATOWN – EVENING

SFX: Chinese musical notes

The cable car stops at the corner of Bush and Grant. The lantern style streetlights in Chinatown are just coming on and the place looks like a magical fairyland, but before MARLIN can disembark from the cable car, RUFE and AARON grab him from behind and pull him off.

MARLIN struggles to escape their hold.

AARON

(shoving some pointed object into Marlin's back)

Just give me an excuse shamus.

When MARLIN is pulled off the cable car, he is seen by CHENG'S older son, PERRY, who is accompanying his dad to the restaurant. CHENG and his son are dressed in 1930's grey suits.

PERRY

(directing his father's attention towards
the alley)

Hey Pop, they got Marlin.

CHENG

You're right. Quick, call Number Two Son and Youngest Daughter.

MARLIN is forced to walk in front of RUFE and AARON. When they turn a corner, DANNY and JASE are waiting.

EXT. CHINATOWN ALLEYWAY / WAREHOUSE – EVENING

RUFE, AARON, DANNY, and JASE drag MARLIN up a sleazy-looking Chinatown back alley then through a human warehouse entrance that leads to a backroom of the gnome section.

INT. BACKROOM OF A WAREHOUSE IN CHINATOWN – EVENING

TOBY

Good Evening Mr. Moto.

MARLIN

I told ya before the name's Marlin.

TOBY

Marlin, Moto, what's the difference? I say your name's trouble and you're gonna own up to it.

DANNY

(while tying Marlin up)

You ain't gonna need no names where you're goin' snooper. We're sending yaz on an all expense paid vacation.

MARLIN

Don't I get to pack?

JASE

Yeah. Take this with ya.

(hits Marlin)

That's a little repayment for the favor you done me.

AARON

With you outta the way Shamus maybe we can take care of that copper's daughter.

MARLIN struggles violently to free himself and they laugh in his face. At that moment The DUCE arrives.

DUCE

Get him up. The boat is ready to sail.

A faint scratching noise is heard in the outer room of the warehouse.

RUFE

What was that?

DUCE

Check it out.

RUFE leaves the room and returns momentarily.

RUFE

There's no one there. It must be rats.

More noise is heard.

DUCE

Come with me. The Shamus isn't goin' anywhere. Spread
out.

While they are out of the room, a panel over MARLIN'S head opens
and PERRY'S head emerges. He is now dressed in a black Kung Fu
outfit.

PERRY

Pssst. Marlin, we got ya covered.

MARLIN

(looking up)

Perry?

PERRY

That's me. Pop and I saw you being nabbed by those mugs.
He sent us over to give ya a hand.

MARLIN

Can you keep a cover on me so I can see who else is involved
in this?

A trapdoor in the floor opens and Number Two Son, ARTHUR, pops out
up to the waist. He is also dressed in a Kung Fu outfit.

ARTHUR

Hi ya Marlin. Don't worry. We got this situation under
control.

MARLIN

Hey Arthur, am I glad to see you guys. Where's Yi Min?

PERRY

She's the one out there making all the noise. Those are some
of the stupidest guys I ever saw. They don't use their heads.
You ever been to college Marlin?

MARLIN

All four years.

PERRY

Yeah me too. Arthur here has two more years and sis starts
next year. You ever read about Socrates?

ARTHUR

The one who drank the poison hemlock.

MARLIN (V.O.)

I couldn't help but compare Cheng's two sons with the boys working me over and suddenly I felt like Socrates, an honest man being condemned for seeking the truth.

The door opens and Duce and the others come back into the room. PERRY and ARTHUR disappear.

RUFE

I told you it was rats.

DANNY

(to Marlin)

Did you miss us?

MARLIN

Yeah, like a bad cold.

TOBY

I hope you speak Chinese, dick, cuz you'll need it in Shanghai.

MARLIN

You guys ever hear about the unexamined life?

JASE

The unexamined what?

RUFE

The shamus is trying to be smart.

AARON

If you're so smart shamus, how come you're the one tied up?

DUCE

Can it. We're wasting time. I'm goin' on ahead. You mugs take him to the docks through the underground passage. Wish him a pleasant trip, and meet me back at the mine.

INT. UNDERGROUND PASSAGE TO DOCKS – EVENING

MARLIN is forced to descend through the same trapdoor from which ARTHUR emerged. From here he is taken to the docks where he is to be dumped into the cargo hold of a Chinese gnome freighter bound for Shanghai.

PERRY, ARTHUR and YI MIN secretly follow the group through the passage by silently scaling overhead pipes and hiding around corners. They give hand signals to each other while causing the gnomes to trip. They also drop loose stones on their heads in order to annoy them and tap on their shoulders. As a result, the gnomes start to bicker among themselves.

RUFE

Lookout! I think the ceiling's coming down.

DANNY

(turning around to look at Jase)

What do you want?

JASE

It wasn't me.

DANNY

(turning around again)

Cut it out Jase.

TOBY

Ouch! Who threw that rock?

AARON

Maybe the shamus is playing games.

MARLIN

Yeah, maybe I got a Gatling gun under my hat.

AARON

Maybe you'd better keep movin' peeper.

Hey! Who pushed me?

TOBY

Get a move on. The Duce is gonna hear about you guys messin' around.

RUFE

It's not us. It's gotta be the shamus.

DANNY

He's got both hands tied. Something's not right about this place.

RUFE

Hey, there's the exit. Let's get outta here.

EXT. WATERFRONT – EVENING

They climb out of the passage and walk along the docks to the boat.

SFX: Fog horn

EXT. BOAT / DECK – EVENING

MARLIN is forced up the ramp and into the gnome boat's cargo hold and TOBY slams shut the hatch bolt.

At the same time, PERRY, ARTHUR, and YI MIN deftly scale the side of the boat and climb aboard. Even though TOBY, AARON, DANNY, RUFE, and JASE do not know Kung Fu, some of the Chinese ship's hands do and a serious fight ensues.

TOBY and AARON attempt to fight off PERRY, ARTHUR, and YI MIN but only look stupid and get themselves beat up in the process.

ARTHUR rolls a knocked out Chinese gnome sailor off the cargo hold hatch and pulls back the bolt to let MARLIN out. Meanwhile, the captain who is preoccupied and oblivious to everything that has happened is now giving orders to set sail.

ARTHUR

C'mon out Marlin, the coast is clear.

MARLIN sticks his head out of the cargo hold.

MARLIN

Are you guys okay?

ARTHUR

Never better.

YI MIN

(with obvious affection for Marlin)

Be careful Marlin. These guys belong to the Barbary Blackbirds. They're a bad lot.

MARLIN

(tipping his hat to Yi Min)

Thanks angel. I'll be careful. Your dad and I still have an appointment to keep with a Peking duck.

(to Arthur)

Which way are we headed?

ARTHUR

Towards the Strait.

MARLIN

(his head still sticking out of the cargo hold)

I think I'll hitch a ride on this junk and grab a ferry at the Presidio. I owe ya a million. Tell your dad I'm grateful.

ARTHUR

Sure thing. By the way, Pop told me to give you a message. He says,

(in Cantonese)

要廢其主幹，先除其黨羽

MARLIN

What does it mean?

PERRY

It means, 'Cut off the branches and the root will die.'

PERRY, ARTHUR, YI MIN, and CHENG who now stands on the dock next to his children say goodbye to MARLIN by exchanging bows with him.

EXT. PRESIDIO – NIGHT

When the boat makes a stop at the Presidio, before heading out to open ocean, MARLIN disembarks and boards a ferry headed across the Strait.

TOBY and AARON, who did not make it off the boat before it set sail for the Presidio, slowly regain consciousness. They discover MARLIN has escaped and quickly disembark. Standing on the dock, they look across the Strait, not realizing that MARLIN is onboard the ferry that is now being swallowed up by the fog and distance.

TOBY

(angrily)

Where is he?

AARON

(intimidated by Toby's temper)

I dun know.

TOBY

The Duce ain't gonna like this.

AARON

Who were those guys?

TOBY

(looking out across the water in Marlin's
direction)

Friends of the shamus.

At the same time, MARLIN is standing on the deck of the ferry looking back at the Presidio still hidden by the fog and distance between him and TOBY.

TOBY (CONT'D)

That guy's got one too many friends if you ask me. But pretty soon there'll be a lot more of us and then we'll see who gets the upper hand.

CUT TO:

INT. SALLY'S PLACE – BEFORE DAWN

MARLIN (V.O.)

It was a few hours before dawn when I arrived at Sally's, cold, wet, hungry, and bruised like a bad banana. B.C. and Sally were still in their nightclothes and fussed over me like a couple of mother hens.

SALLY pours MARLIN a drink and B.C. brings him some dry clothes.

MARLIN (V.O.) (CONT'D)

I knew I had to find some real answers and that somehow the Blackbird was at the bottom of things. It was time to go underground, but first I needed to grab a few hours sleep and then spend a little of that time alone with B.C.

MARLIN emerges from a backroom at Sallys and discovers B.C. sitting on the floor in front of the fireplace waiting for him. He sits in a club chair across from her.

MARLIN

They're lookin' for ya B.C..

B.C.

If it wasn't for me you wouldn't be involved in this.

MARLIN

Come on honey, you know better than that. This case has been heatin' up so fast; I'd have been in it sooner or later anyway. I gotta go underground and I want you to be especially careful while I'm gone. They know you're here.

B.C.

Let me go with you.

MARLIN

Not this time.

B.C.

What've you found out so far? Who are those guys?

MARLIN

That's just it. They're nobody special, just some ordinary gnomes, town bullies, the usual criminal riffraff. I can't figure it. The odd thing is that their numbers are increasing so fast. Parks can't figure it either.

B.C.

You mean they're recruiting people?

MARLIN

Yeah.

MARLIN (V.O.)

I didn't tell B.C. about the symbol of the blackbird. If she was caught and interrogated . . . the less information she had the better. Being Phil's daughter, she had a good head on her shoulders. For now, Sally's would be as safe a place as any.

(beat)

For a few minutes neither of us said anything. We listened to the logs crackle in the fireplace and were surrounded by the warmth and retreat-like atmosphere of Sally's hospitality. B.C. was the first to break the silence.

B.C.

Do you think it's ever too late? I mean for people who spend their whole lives making bad choices.

MARLIN

I guess that depends on what they want outta life.

B.C.

My dad used to tell me that if he didn't think people could change, he was in the wrong line of work.

MARLIN

We all make choices baby. But the thing a lot of people don't realize is that life makes a few choices of its own. We gotta own up to that.

B.C.

Take care of yourself underground.

MARLIN (V.O.)

We exchange a look of farewell. I stand in the doorway and adjust my hat trying to find some excuse not to leave. I take a last look at B.C. sitting on the floor by the fire, turn towards the night, and close the door behind me. My destination – the pixie encampment.

Meanwhile, gnomes are seen making their way to the mine by various routes through the sewers and across the water.

INT. INSIDE THE MINE – BEFORE DAWN

Underground, the gnomes are gathering around the Barbary Blackbird, a statue made from carved onyx. Its wingtips are inlaid with rubies and its eyes with emeralds. There is a brazier in the center of the cave and torches line the walls. The only adornment worn by many in the group is the Barbary Blackbird armband.

The initiation ritual begins. One-by-one several new gnome recruits approach a table covered with a beige cloth displaying the Barbary Blackbird emblem and receive their armbands. The DUCE sits behind the table and ceremoniously hands out the armbands while TOBY, who is seated next to him, records their names in a book.

DUCE gets up to speak.

DUCE

As a Blackbird, you are free to think for yourself to make your own choices . . . to control your destiny. We will show you the way and together we will shape your future.

RUFE

(to Aaron)

I'm a little confused.

AARON

Yeah, me too. I'm not sure I get it.

JASE

(whirling around to face them)

Shhhh! Be quiet you guys, I'm tryin' to listen. He's tellin' us how to think for ourselves.

AARON

(looking at Rufe with a how-do-ya-figure expression)

Sure Jase, sure.

DANNY

(looking in Toby's direction)

Toby's done okay for himself.

RUFE

(straining to see Toby over the top of the crowd)

Doesn't look too happy though.

GNOMES IN THE CROWD

Shhhh!!

CUT TO:

EXT. PIXIE ENCAMPMENT – EARLY MORNING

SFX: Hauntingly beautiful gypsy-like music

NOTE: The Muir Woods pixies are a combination of fairy and gypsy-elf. They are only slightly smaller in stature than the gnomes and have iridescent wings that lay flat on their backs. Some are fair, dark or olive-skinned.

In spite of their nomadic lifestyle, the pixies are actually a highly sophisticated, knowledgeable and secretive community. Experience has taught them to be on their guard against outsiders. And although they are shrewd in their dealings with others, they are also compassionate and uncompromisingly loyal in friendship.

MARLIN (V.O.)

It was early morning by the time I reached the pixie encampment. I was greeted by Pyxis, the head of the clan. Pyxis was a lookout for Phil and me on our last job. If there was one thing the three of us had in common — it was that last trip underground. Pyxis had almost lost an eye and took a bullet in the wing; and if anyone had a favor coming to him, it was Pyxis. But all I needed this time was a little information.

MARLIN and PYXIS embrace and are quickly surrounded by smiling pixie children who take MARLIN by each hand and escort him into the camp. Afterward, the children run off as quickly as they appeared.

PYXIS, the head of the clan, is a noble looking figure with a small scar over his right eye.

PYXIS

(in the Romany-Pixie language to a member of his clan, subtitled in English)

Some refreshment for our friend. . . .

(placing his hand on Marlin's back)

Let us celebrate our reunion.

MARLIN and PYXIS sit on benches in front of a fire and are each handed a tankard of a steaming hot, invigorating beverage. The pixie encampment is filled with beautifully ornate gypsy-like wagons that are invisible to humans. The scene includes shots of the encampment and its inhabitants as well as PYXIS and MARLIN in conversation.

PYXIS (CONT'D)

You'd better talk to the Pixie Sisters. They keep a close watch on the old mine entrance. They can tell you more about these strange events than I can. In the meantime, tell me the news of the City by the Bay.

MARLIN (V.O.)

After about an hour, refreshed and in good spirits, I left the pixie encampment and headed north along a familiar route towards the entrance of an old abandoned goldmine.

EXT. MINE ENTRANCE – EARLY MORNING

MARLIN (V.O.) (CONT'D)

On my arrival, I notice that the framed cave-like entrance of the mine is overhung with moss and vines and that the top is covered by a small grassy mound. The Pixie Sisters, Petals and Iris, are sitting on top of the entrance sunning themselves, swinging their legs back and forth, sassy faces turned to the sun. Carefree and relaxed, they remind me of a work by Maxfield Parrish.

MARLIN

(coolly tipping his hat)

What's the news ladies?

The Pixie Sisters eye MARLIN suspiciously and momentarily seem to ignore him.

IRIS

What's it to ya?

MARLIN

Look sister, I'm trying to be civil. I just want to know if you've seen any action around the entrance to this mine lately.

PETALS

It's like my sister said, What's it to ya?

MARLIN

Come on down here and I'll show ya.

IRIS

(to Petals)

We ain't seen nothin' worth yappin' about, have we sister?

The sisters wink at one another and jump down. MARLIN is not sure whether they mean to run or attack him. He grabs IRIS by the wings. PETALS is stunned by his quick action.

MARLIN

Now look sister, you'd better talk to me or what's good for you will be good for your sister.

PETALS

Ok bud, lay off, we'll sing. We seen a few mugs goin' in and outta here around sunset. But they ain't never seen us cuz we hide when we see 'em.

MARLIN

How come you ladies didn't hide when you saw me?

IRIS

(now free of Marlin's grasp)

We saw ya, but you didn't look like the bullying type. You turned out to be a real tough guy.

(to Petals)

Didn't he sis? A lousy knothole peeper!

PETALS

(to Marlin)

Yeah. Next time pick on somebody your own size sapshoe!

After they talk, he lets the Sisters go. They fly off looking back and calling him names that cannot be clearly heard as their voices trail off into the distance.

INT. INSIDE THE MINE – EARLY MORNING

MARLIN enters the mine and after a short walk begins a descent.

MARLIN (V.O.)

I knew this place. Down here a man could find the answers to almost anything if he had courage enough to make the trip. I first came with B.C.'S old man, after that I ventured here on my own. Only it had nothing to do with being a detective; it was personal.

MARLIN comes to an unfamiliar passage.

MARLIN

(aloud)

I don't remember this turn. There must have been a cave in.

SFX: Muffled conversation.

MARLIN turns off his flashlight and takes the path..

DUCE

I know I saw a light over here. One of you was supposed to be watching the entrance.

MARLIN (V.O.)

Darkness closed in around me and the air grew increasingly colder. This was the realm of the goblins and the trolls. And in spite of their dark suits and silk ties, the gargoyled faces of these creatures could only be described as chipped granite.

(beat)

MARLIN (V.O.) (CONT'D)

I began to wonder why I decided to come here at all. Then I remembered B.C.. Where were those guys going? Should I be following them? A little voice in my head told me to stay right where I was, so I followed my instincts and kept to the path. After what seemed like hours, I felt a cool breeze and the path began to widen. There was a yellow shaft of light and the sound of running water.

Then suddenly, the path ended and I was no longer in the passage.

INT. MINE – UNDERGROUND CATHEDRAL – DAY

The passage comes to an abrupt end and MARLIN finds himself in what can only be described as an underground cathedral.

The ceiling is vaulted and although the structure is natural, it is reminiscent of the Art Deco décor present throughout the film. Sunlight filters through openings in the roof and upper walls and is reflected against quartz crystal and naturally polished stone creating an unimaginable array of colors and brilliance.

The walls of the cavern are warm, alive, and vibrant. The stalagmites and stalactites are like carved columns with some joined in the middle and reaching from floor to ceiling seemingly hundreds of feet above MARLIN'S head. The ground is made of polished stone. Here and there, water trickles from small rivulets.

MARLIN walks out towards the middle of the cavern cathedral. From overhead, he appears only a few inches tall in relation to its enormous size. He removes his fedora and looks up.

MARLIN

(aloud)

Makes a guy feel awful small.

CUT TO:

INT. SALLY'S PLACE – DAY

While MARLIN is underground, customers at Sally's are ordering lunch. One of them is a middle-aged woman accompanied by her elderly father, an OLD MAN in a wheelchair. They are seated at one of the tables, waiting to be served.

OLD MAN

(mumbling explicatives)

@#$%!, @#$%!, @#$%!

DAUGHTER

Don't mumble Papa.

(to waitress)

My dad will have a bowl of soup and I will have the chicken salad with –

RUFE, TOBY, AARON, DANNY, and JASE suddenly burst into Sally's and begin to throw things around.

AARON

(addresses Sally)

Okay sister, where are you hiding that dame?

B.C. ducks behind a counter but hears everything that is going on. She makes an effort to come out and help SALLY, but LOLA holds her back. RUFE, DANNY, TOBY, AARON, and JASE are knocking over tables, chairs and bottles.

LOLA

Listen B.C., you can't go out there. Sally knows what she's doing. This isn't the first time she's handled that sort. Sally's got a friend underground and believe me they're only gonna go just so far if they know what's good for 'em.

B.C.

Okay. But there must be something we can do.

No sooner are the words out of her mouth when the OLD MAN begins to mumble very loudly.

OLD MAN

(mumbling explicatives)

@#$%!, @#$%!, @#$%!

And as if he is suddenly imbued with super-gnome power from a mysterious source, he thrusts his wheelchair away from the table and heads slam-bang for DANNY.

DAUGHTER

Papa! Where are you going?

He crashes into DANNY'S shins. DANNY screams and doubles over. Then he heads for RUFE and backs him into a corner. He rears his wheelchair up like a horse intending to charge into RUFE'S shins. RUFE lets out a yell anticipating the impact. The OLD MAN moves like lightening. And for an instant, the OLD MAN'S head transfigures into the translucent shape of a dragon's head and back again.

TOBY

Jase, take him out.

JASE

I can't do that! He's an old man.

TOBY

(standing in the path of the rampaging chair)

Well I can.

The OLD MAN suddenly backs up, runs into AARON and rolls over TOBY'S feet. Limping in pain, TOBY goes for the OLD MAN forcing him to back up towards the counter where B.C. is hiding. B.C. grabs a pot while remaining concealed and raises her arm to throw it at TOBY. But surprisingly, the OLD MAN reaches up from behind, grabs the pot from B.C. and hits TOBY over the head.

TOBY is knocked silly and the gnomes decide to leave the place immediately. On their way out, AARON shoves a table out of his way and inadvertently breaks the plate glass window. The OLD MAN returns to his place and waits patiently for his soup to be brought.

CUT TO:

INT. MINE – UNDERGROUND CATHEDRAL – DAY

MARLIN continues to look around and is awed by the grandeur of the cathedral.

MARLIN (V.O.)

There was nowhere to hide; that place showed a fellah his whole life, if only he let himself remember. On the other side of the cathedral, I found the entrance to another tunnel. This time the ground was level. I used my hand along the wall instead of my flashlight. I followed the path for about a quarter of a mile and could just make out a faint light in the distance. It was accompanied by an unmistakable breeze. It had a smoky fragrance that reminded me of a eucalyptus forest after an autumn rain. I knew then that I was on the right path and that I had reached my destination, Anthony's cave.

INT. MINE – ANTHONY'S STUDY – DAY

SFX: Inviting crackle of logs burning in fireplace

MARLIN enters a large, homey, castle-like room. Here the light comes from a candlelit chandelier and torch-like lights along the walls. There is a magnificent polished stone fireplace with a wide mantle. The room is carpeted in oriental rugs and furnished as a comfortable study.

Books line tall shelves and are stacked on tables. A cut glass decanter and glasses are arranged on a silver tray on top of a mahogany sideboard.

Light beams are seen coming from openings high above that let in fresh air. In the center of the room, enveloped by the glow of the fireplace, sits a colossal, very handsome, blue-green dragon curled comfortably before the fire, apparently engrossed in reading.

MARLIN enters the room.

MARLIN

Hello Anthony.

The dragon raises his head but not in a preoccupied or surprised way, but with complete presence of mind and concentration on the speaker. He greets MARLIN in a familiar and affectionate manner.

ANTHONY

(removing his pince-nez)

Jackie. It's been a very long time by your years. Come in and make yourself comfortable.

(pointing to a chair by the fire)

Here, sit by me.

MARLIN

You know why I have come.

ANTHONY

What is it you want to know?

MARLIN

I'm lookin' out for a certain young lady.

ANTHONY

Our friend, Phil's girl. I've watched her grow up.

MARLIN

There's a lot more goin' on here than just a wave of petty crime and I believe it's connected with the underground.

ANTHONY

You're a good detective Marlin, but this case is gonna take more than brains to solve.

MARLIN

Where do I begin?

ANTHONY

You're curious about the blackbird. That's where you begin.

MARLIN

Is it some kinda cult?

ANTHONY

The bird itself has no significance. Those who believe in it give it power.

MARLIN

And if the blackbird is found and destroyed?

ANTHONY

No. Destroying the bird will not make any difference. Do you know what sacrifice is?

MARLIN

I suppose it's when someone gives up something that means a lot.

ANTHONY

It's when you're alone, outnumbered, and no one knows what it will cost you. That's the price. When there is no one to cheer you, and you meet yourself in the silence.

(beat)

When the time comes Jackie, you'll know what to do. Now, let's have a drink together.

CUT TO:

INT. MINE – LATE AFTERNOON

MARLIN (V.O.)

I bid my farewell to Anthony and started back along the path towards the entrance of the mine. I knew somehow I didn't need to investigate any further underground for the time being. I also knew what realm lay adjacent to the hallowed halls of the dragon. I would be returning to the mine before long and it wouldn't be a social visit. Anthony made it clear that the next time I entered the mine, I wouldn't need my gun.

CUT TO:

INT. SALLY'S PLACE – EARLY EVENING

MARLIN arrives at Sally's and finds the place ransacked. SALLY and B.C. are putting things back in order. They see MARLIN and come out to greet him.

MARLIN (V.O.) (CONT'D)

When I got back to Sally's, my heart skipped a beat. The place was a mess.

(beat)

I could see the lights shining through a broken window-pane. B.C. came out to meet me. The moment I saw her it all began to make sense. There were some things in life worth sacrificing for and we both knew it.

SALLY

(broom in hand)

Marlin! Am I glad to see you. I called a couple of the boys and asked them to stick around till we get this thing settled. I mean you got us all involved in it this time.

MARLIN and B.C. look at one another.

MARLIN

I know Sally.

EXT. OUTSIDE SALLY'S PLACE – EVENING

The band is playing background music. MARLIN and B.C. are walking outside and seat themselves at an outdoor table with a small candlelit lantern in the center.

MARLIN

Have you ever been underground B.C.?

B.C.

A few times with my dad when I was a child. He said he wanted to show me a wonderful place I would never forget.

MARLIN

I know the place. Have you met Anthony?

B.C.

Yes, when I was very young. My father used to speak of him as the Wise One who lives underground. Whenever he spoke his name I wanted to return there. Did you see him?

MARLIN

Yes.

B.C.

There are other places underground.

MARLIN

Yeah, your dad and I have been there.

B.C.

I know. You almost lost your life there once. I'm afraid for you Marlin.

SALLY comes over to their table. MARLIN rises and starts to pull out a chair out for her.

SALLY

(waving her hand)

No, no. I just wanted to see how you were doing.

MARLIN

(finishing his drink and putting on his hat)

You two take care.

MARLIN'S disappears into the foggy wood as he makes his way back to the City.

CUT TO:

INT. SALLY'S PLACE – B.C.'S BEDROOM – NIGHT

B.C. has a dream she is finding her way to the mine. She wakes up and quietly leaves Sally's.

EXT. MUIR WOODS – NIGHT

She passes the pixie encampment unseen by a group of gnomes going past her.

INT. MINE – NIGHT

She enters the mine and takes a torch from the wall. After walking for a while, she hears voices and sees firelight ahead, then takes the same alternate path as MARLIN, leading to the underground cathedral.

INT. MINE – UNDERGROUND CATHEDRAL – NIGHT

Since it is night, the cathedral cavern is lit only by the torch in her hand.

As she passes through the cathedral, looking up at the massive walls and ceiling, she recalls her visits there with her father when she was a child.

MEMORY FLASHBACK – B.C. as a child holding her father's hand standing in the middle of the cathedral.

BACK TO SCENE

> **B.C.**
>
> (aloud)

I remember this place.

She continues her journey, seemingly guided by a mysterious force, and arrives at ANTHONY'S cave. And although the dragon seems to be napping before the fireplace, she discovers he is expecting her.

> **ANTHONY**

Come in B.C. You were just a child the last time we met.

> **B.C.**

I had to come.

> **ANTHONY**

Yes, I know.

> **B.C.**

I want to help Marlin. I'm afraid for him.

> **ANTHONY**

What about the cause you're fighting for?

> **B.C.**

Am I a part of it?

ANTHONY

That's up to you. There's all kinds of people in this world and they all have choices to make, but when it comes down to it there is only one choice that really means anything.

B.C.

What's that?

ANTHONY

The choice for Good.

B.C.

My dad used to tell me he lived by a code of honor.

(in Japanese subtitled in English)

To give one's life for the cause of life.

ANTHONY

(with reverence)

Yes. And he lived by that code even through his last illness.

B.C.

What can I do to help?

Instead of answering her question, he tells her his own history and about the association between himself, PHIL and MARLIN, and by way of this explanation, communicates to B.C. how a person can decide to risk all for a noble cause – the hardest of all choices.

ANTHONY

(musingly with pride)

The three of us, your dad, Marlin, and me. . . .

(beat)

ANTHONY (CONT'D)

We made a great team.

(focusing on B.C.)

Did he ever tell you how we met?

B.C.

He told me a few stories . . .

ANTHONY

Next to me is the realm of the goblins and trolls. They are full of mischief and spend their time rabblerousing among the gnomes and humans.

B.C.

The underground creatures.

ANTHONY

Yes. And although they are no threat to me, they never tire of luring the weak-minded to join their numbers. Yet I can assure you they have no special liking for gnomes. I have been here a very long time and will remain as long as necessary. I belong to an ancient order, one of those whose task it is to observe and give counsel . . .

(emphasis)

and assistance.

B.C.

That is how you know things.

ANTHONY

Your dad sought my advice before you were born. We had many long talks together. He sat in that very chair.

(beat)

At the dragon's words, B.C.'s expression loses some of its sadness.

ANTHONY (CONT'D)

And he introduced me to Marlin.

(wistfully)

Those were the days, full of adventure, though not the kind, I dare say, most people would welcome. It seems to me we are fast approaching a similar time.

B.C.

And now I have come.

ANTHONY

Yes.

(beat)

And we will meet again in the future.

(beat)

You know, courage is more about sacrifice than victory. Real courage means doing the right thing for the right reason.

B.C.

Anthony, what's going to happen to Marlin?

ANTHONY

(encouragingly)

When you return, give Sally my regards.

B.C. smiles at ANTHONY through teary eyes as he escorts her to the entrance of his cave. He gives her a look that comforts her and lays his dragon's paw on her shoulder. She momentarily rests her forehead on his chest then leaves.

CUT TO:

INT. MARLIN'S OFFICE / BATHROOM – EARLY MORNING

MARLIN arrives at his office.

MARLIN (V.O.)

It was sometime after midnight when I arrived back at my office for a long drink and a quick shave. I found Ivy waiting for me in the outer room. She had a large bruise on the left side of her face and looked just as scared.

IVY

I did a stupid thing Marlin.

MARLIN

You mean Toby? He's a real nice guy alright. What do ya tell him when he comes to dinner? Hang up your coat and lay your chain on the table?

IVY

Yeah. I never should've given that jerk the time of day and if the cops catch up with him I might be in real trouble.

MARLIN

(gently touching her face)

Looks like you got a face full of trouble already.

IVY

I've been doin' some thinking. . . . It's not the first time he's slugged me.

MARLIN talks to IVY in a raised voice while he shaves in the bathroom.

MARLIN

That's usually the way of it. There's a bottle in the top drawer. . . .

(points)

Pour us both a drink and tell me what I can do for you.

IVY

I haven't got any money. But I'm not gonna sell myself cheap anymore neither. Marlin, I gotta get out of the City. I heard you got B.C. out.

MARLIN comes out of the bathroom in a sleeveless undershirt and talks to IVY while drying his face.

MARLIN

How do I know you're not puttin' the wool over?

He tosses the towel around his neck and takes the drink she offers him.

IVY

Cuz you know I'm not.

MARLIN (V.O.)

She was right. I did know. Cuz I knew her type, as ignorant as an acorn and as love starved as an orphan in winter. She was the type to always have that pretty face of hers stuck in the mirror. Now look at it. She was also one of those dames who always fell for some jerk just because he was pretty and pitiful. But she knew I'd help her, not because I felt sorry for her, but because for once in her life she was being honest with herself.

(beat)

I called Sally and then Parks. He arranged to have one of his men secretly escort Ivy across the water.

MARLIN

(eyeing her battered valise)

Have you got any clothes with ya?

IVY

Yeah, everything I own is in this little bag. I left the stuff Toby bought me.

MARLIN

Okay sister.

(holding the door for her)

Let's get goin'.

MARLIN accompanies IVY and NICK to the Presidio.

MARLIN (V.O.)

It was already sunrise when Ivy and Nick boarded the ferry.

CUT TO:

EXT. MINE ENTRANCE – EARLY MORNING

B.C. meets the Pixie Sisters as she emerges from the mine at sunrise. She has regained her composure and is on her way back to Sally's.

IRIS

Hey honey, you look like you could use some sunshine. My name's Iris. This is my sister Petals.

PETALS

(extending a slim, little leg and admiring
her tan)

There's room for a third if you care to join us.

B.C.

(looking up)

Oh, hi.

IRIS

You're brave goin' in there. Hey, aren't you that Sweet Pea who's been stayin' at Sally's?

B.C.

My name's B.C.. You won't tell anyone you've seen me will you?

PETALS

B.C. honey, if we told the things we saw comin' in and outta of this place our lives wouldn't be worth a nickel. We only talked to the snooper cuz he beat it out of us.

B.C. knows they are talking about MARLIN and lowers her head to hide a smile as she departs.

PETALS (CONT'D)

(to Iris)

Seems like a nice kid.

IRIS

Yeah, only two kinds a people ever go in or outta this place . . .

(beat)

the very brave and the very stupid.

PETALS

Which one do you think she is, Sister?

CUT TO:

INT. SALLY'S PLACE – MORNING

SALLY is standing outside catching some early morning sun when IVY arrives escorted by NICK.

SALLY

So you're Ivy. I think we can find some room for you here.

(addressing Nick)

Congratulations! Marlin tells me you had a girl.

NICK

Thanks. She looks just like her mama.

SALLY

It's been awhile Nick, why don't you come in for a sandwich.

NICK

I told the Chief I'd be right back. You know how he worries. Maybe another time.

IVY holds out her hand to the young officer.

IVY

Thanks for everything.

NICK takes her hand, tips his cap to both women, and leaves.

IVY (CONT'D)

(to Sally)

Is there anything I can do to repay you and Marlin?

SALLY

How'd you like a job? Marlin tells me you're ready to turn over a new leaf.

IVY

Yes Mam. I am.

CUT TO:

B.C. is sitting at a table by herself listening to LOLA sing in the background. SALLY comes over and sits across from her.

B.C.

(addressing Sally)

I don't think I have any special talents.

SALLY

B.C., you yourself are the gift and Marlin knows it.

IVY approaches the table with a frightened expression on her face. SALLY looks up and invites her to join them.

SALLY (CONT'D)

C'mon sit down. We're like a family here. What's on your mind?

IVY

I gotta funny feeling. I keep thinking about Marlin.

SALLY

Yeah, I know what you mean.

B.C. looks worried and IVY puts an arm around her.

DISSOLVE TO:

EXT. PRESIDIO – EVENING

MARLIN (V.O.)

The rest of that day I hung around the Presidio. I wanted to make sure Ivy wasn't being followed. I walked along the beach and looked out across the Strait at the bridge still under construction . . . and I watched the sunset over the Bay. Then I boarded a ferry and secretly returned to Muir Woods.

MONTAGE

EXT. MUIR WOODS – MINE – NIGHT

1) MARLIN returns to Muir Woods that same night. An icy wet wind lashes his cheeks and stings his eyes forcing him to turn up the collar of his raincoat. A jagged bolt of lightening shoots across his path and thunder cracks menacingly overhead. As he approaches Sally's, he is careful to avoid being spotted by SALLY'S hired gnome bodyguards.

2) MARLIN checks on B.C. by looking through a window. He watches her say goodnight to SALLY and IVY.

3) MARLIN makes his way past the pixie encampment. He sees twinkling lights hanging from the wagons and hears the haunting pixie music. His expression shows that he longs for PYXIS' companionship rather than go underground.

INTERCUT BETWEEN MARLIN AND THE GROUP UNDERGROUND

4) Below, deep in the mine, the renegade gnomes, goblins and trolls are gathering around the statue of the Barbary Blackbird. Lights from a large brazier and torches are reflected on the wall. Yet the shadowy forms they reveal appear far more sinister than the actual figures in the cave. The DUCE is seated at his table with TOBY next to him. They are preparing to dispatch armbands to a group of gnome recruits standing at attention.

5) Intercuts move back and forth between MARLIN walking through the stormy woods at night and the activity underground. As he leaves the pixie encampment behind and moves deeper into the woods, the last fading strains of a pixie melody can be heard.

6) Upon his arrival at the mine, all is quiet except for the sound of the rain and windswept leaves. MARLIN takes a torch left in the wall and goes straight to the underground chamber where the renegade gnomes, goblins, and trolls are located.

SONG: Music and lyrics that generate the same tenor of emotion and sentiment as Bonnie Tyler's original version of "Holding Out for a Hero".

INTERCUT BETWEEN MARLIN AND B.C.

7) MARLIN enters the mine. Back at Sally's, B.C. is sitting up in her bed looking worried and sensing that something is wrong. She is unable to sleep.

8) Intercuts continue to move back and forth between MARLIN'S cautious descent into the mine and B.C..

9) The renegade gnomes, goblins, and trolls are shocked and incredulous to discover that MARLIN has entered their underground chamber and that he has come unarmed except for his fists. The goblins become increasingly infuriated by MARLIN'S act of courage and daring.

10) Goaded by DUCE, the group mocks him with a roar of garbled shouts and flies at him in a rage.

11) MARLIN fights them off.

12) AARON, DANNY, RUFE, and JASE and some of the other renegade gnomes gradually move away from the crunch and look on with expressions of disbelief. Some of the trolls also stand back looking stupid while the goblins incite the gnomes to join in the fight.

13) MARLIN fights with courage and determination. A couple of renegade gnomes jump in again and fight with the goblins against MARLIN.

SONG: Continues to play

INTERCUT BETWEEN MARLIN AND B.C.

14) MARLIN is tiring. He is taking an awful beating, but he is giving more than he gets. There are renegade gnomes, goblins, and trolls knocked out or sprawling all over the floor.

15) B.C.'s expression shows that she feels everything MARLIN is going through. She knows that MARLIN'S life is in danger.

SFX: Thunder and lightening

16) The fight is also revealed by the shadows on the walls and by the sounds of the storm going on outside the mine. Sometimes when MARLIN gets

punched or punches someone else, instead of the sound of the punch, a thunder crack can be heard.

EXT. AERIAL VIEW OF MUIR WOODS / STRAIT / CITY – NIGHT

17) The shot moves upward from the cave, across the Strait, and over the lighted City.

SFX: Gunshots and police sirens

Intercuts between the fight in the cave and the aerial view over the City show PARKS and his men, CHARLIE, NICK, JOHNNY, and LUKE, on the beat chasing bad guys. Under the glow of street lamps and neon signs, the nighttime city comes alive.

18) SHERWOOD and his family are awakened from their sleep. Their expressions of worry reveal they know something is wrong with MARLIN.

19) CLAUDINE and CHESTER, asleep on the porch, wakeup and look at one another. They too know MARLIN is in trouble. CHESTER is still wearing his doggie trench coat and badly crumpled fedora.

20) As the aerial shot continues to move over the City, the waking expressions of BUSTER and then GRIS reveal their anxiety for MARLIN.

21) Finally, the shot moves back over the Strait to Muir Woods and to Sally's. SALLY is standing looking out the window at the rain. Her expression shows that she also knows.

22) The shot then focuses on B.C.. A few tears roll down her cheek.

23) PYXIS is seen standing in the pixie encampment, arms folded, looking worriedly at the fire.

INT. MINE – NIGHT

24) MARLIN is down, flat on his face and struggles to get up, but it is no use. DUCE approaches him and his body tenses in anticipation of a sharp kick from the DUCE'S knife-edged wingtips but the kick never comes. In front of the other renegade gnomes DUCE takes off his gnome costume to reveal that he is actually a hideous, hairy goblin.

25) MARLIN'S P.O.V. – Painfully, MARLIN gets on his feet again and with a sudden burst of energy and the two engage in a brutal struggle. For an instant, the room dissolves and they appear to be outside of time. Then MARLIN is back again and unable to catch his breath. But just at that moment, it seems as if a spell starts to break.

26) Some of the renegade gnomes run out of the mine because they can no longer bear to watch the fight. DANNY, RUFE, AARON, and JASE now faced with the reality of what they are involved in look at each other as if to say, "What have we been doing?" and try to defend MARLIN, but they are outnumbered and held back by the trolls and goblins. They decide to flee rather than suffer MARLIN'S fate.

27) Only TOBY, who has gotten a beating from MARLIN, remains in the mine and goads on the attack.

28) One of the trolls backs into the statue of the Blackbird and knocks it over. The statue topples onto the ground and the goblins are temporarily distracted. MARLIN is down again. DUCE looks around and finds that most of the gnomes have fled.

DUCE

(without his gnome costume)

Leave him; he's finished. There'll be another time.

29) Defeated because his deception is exposed, DUCE decides to leave MARLIN for dead and move into the deeper recesses of the cave along with some of the gnomes who choose to remain.

30) TOBY looks around and hesitates for a moment as if he is trying to decide whether to ascend to the surface or retreat further underground with DUCE. The scene blackens and his final choice remains a mystery.

END MONTAGE

CUT TO:

INT. SALLY'S PLACE – DAWN

B.C. is still sitting up in her bed. But now she has resolute expression. She turns her head and looks out the window through the trees and at the path that leads in the direction of the mine. The woods are grey and foggy in the pale dawn light.

CUT TO:

EXT. MINE ENTRANCE – EARLY MORNING

B.C. and IVY arrive together at the mine. Their faces are tear-stained and their appearance disheveled.

PETALS and IRIS are sunning themselves as usual, but their carefree countenances change as soon as they see B.C. and IVY coming towards them. B.C. exchanges glances with the Pixie Sisters and they immediately jump off the entrance and go with them into the mine to rescue MARLIN.

INT. INSIDE THE MINE – MORNING

The women discover MARLIN lying face down in the dirt on the floor of the cave. No one is in sight and the place looks eerie. The only light emanates from a few torches left in the wall and the dying embers in the brazier. From their expressions, it is obvious they are uncomfortable. They struggle to drag MARLIN out of the mine and into the sunshine.

EXT. MINE ENTRANCE – MORNING

MARLIN momentarily regains consciousness.

MARLIN

(weakly)

B.C. . . .

(blacks out again)

IRIS

(to B.C., IVY, and PETALS)

Let's take him to Pyxis.

The women take MARLIN to PYXIS so that he can treat his injuries. Although he is in and out of consciousness, he notices that the woods are wet and glistening after the night's rain and seem to be alive with magic. Sunlight filters down in shafts through the trees, sparkles on the surfaces of leaves, and is refracted in rainbow colors from droplets clinging to lacy cobwebs.

EXT. PIXIE ENCAMPMENT – MORNING

When they arrive at the grove of sheltering trees surrounding the pixie encampment, the women lay MARLIN on an elevated bed of soft, dry groundcover and gossamer silks. Then they slowly draw away as PYXIS approaches. The scene becomes dreamlike and slowly fades showing the back of PYXIS standing over MARLIN.

CUT TO:

INT. TOBY'S APARTMENT – MORNING

AARON, JASE, RUFE, and DANNY talk among themselves about the events of the previous night.

JASE

Toby didn't come back.

AARON

Maybe he stayed underground.

RUFE

I never liked the way he was smackin' Ivy around.

DANNY

Do you think Marlin's still alive?

RUFE

I don't know. Those guys might have killed him.

JASE

What are we gonna do?

DANNY

I'm going back to see if I can find him.

AARON

Yeah, but if those underground guys are still there. . . .

DANNY

I'm tired of being stupid. The Duce wasn't even one of us.

(takes off his armband and throws it across
the room)

JASE

Yeah, me too.

      (takes off his armband and throws it in the
          same way)

Let's go.

      (to Aaron and Rufe)

Are you guys coming?

RUFE and AARON quickly take off their armbands and follow DANNY and JASE.

      CUT TO:

INT. UNDERGROUND CAVE – AFTERNOON

By the time they arrive at the mine, MARLIN has already been taken away and the cave is completely deserted. Only the toppled statue of the Blackbird lies in the dust on the floor.

DANNY

Look!

      (kicks the blackbird)

JASE

Marlin's gone.

RUFE

      (anxiously)

What do we do now?

AARON

I wish I'd never got into this business.

DANNY

(resolutely)

Let's go to Sally's.

RUFE

Sally's!!

DANNY

You got a better suggestion?

They look back and forth at one another as if to say, "Well, where else can we go?".

CUT TO:

INT. SALLY'S PLACE – LATE AFTERNOON

DANNY, AARON, RUFE, and JASE arrive at Sally's afraid and full of shame. They hesitate at the entrance and do not go inside. She greets them at the door and observes their demeanor.

SALLY

(knowingly with stern compassion)

What is it you four want?

They hang their heads and do not answer.

SALLY (CONT'D)

So that's how it is. Yes, he's here.

Although their reaction to SALLY'S words show they are surprised and greatly relieved to learn that MARLIN is still alive and staying at Sally's, an expression of guilt and shame quickly returns to their faces.

SALLY (CONT'D)

I guess he could use a little cheering up. C'mon in.

She escorts them to a back bedroom with everyone looking on in disbelief since they are the same gnomes that caused a ruckus in the place days earlier.

INT. BACK BEDROOM AT SALLY'S PLACE – LATE AFTERNOON

Through the open doorway MARLIN is seen lying in bed with his arm in a sling and a bandage on his head covered over by his gnome cap.

SALLY (CONT'D)

(putting her head in the room)

You up to some company Marlin?

MARLIN nods in ascent and his eyes meet those of the four gnomes. They take off the hats they wear over their gnome caps as they enter the room. SALLY closes the door and the gnomes remain with Marlin for a little while.

BC, IVY, and Ricky are seen casually talking among themselves without audio. Ricky is behind the bar and the activity at Sally's goes on as usual.

There is a spectacular shot of the sunset and view of the woods through the newly replaced plate glass window which is being polished by a gnome worker in overalls.

JASE, AARON, DANNY, and RUFE come out of MARLIN'S room in a still somber, but now somewhat relieved attitude and head for the main door.

SALLY (CONT'D)

What's your hurry fellahs? Soup's on.

The four gnomes look surprised and grateful for the invitation. A light comes into their faces and replaces the somber attitude. They seat themselves together at a table. The band plays, IVY serves them, and LOLA sings something soft in the background.

DANNY

(to Jase with a thoughtful expression)

What was that you asked Marlin?

JASE

I asked him if he could teach me more about the examined life.

RUFE

(reaching for a breadstick)

You mean the unexamined life.

AARON

(looking at him inquisitively over the top of his salad)

What's he talking about?

RUFE

I think that's how he beat The Duce.

DANNY

(tearing off a slice of French bread and busily buttering it)

Maybe he knows something we don't.

AARON

Are you trying to say we don't know everything?

DANNY

(putting his knife down with a smile of
cheerful resignation)

Yeah.

CUT TO:

MARLIN'S P.O.V. – He recaps his rescue from the mine.

INT. FLASHBACK – INSIDE MINE – MORNING

MARLIN (V.O.)

I didn't know how I made it back to Sally's. I vaguely remembered being shoved and pulled up a hill. There were
voices. . . . I thought I was dreaming.

EXT. FLASHBACK – MINE ENTRANCE – MORNING

MARLIN is dragged slowly out of the mine and laid on the grass at the
entrance by IVY, B.C., PETALS, and IRIS. They carefully turn him over
onto his back.

MARLIN (V.O.) (CONT'D)

The next thing I knew was the taste of clover and the face
of B.C. bending over me.

MARLIN

B.C. . . .

MARLIN (V.O.) (CONT'D)

But before she could answer, I blacked out.

DISSOLVE TO:

EXT. MARLIN'S FRONT LAWN – NIGHT

MARLIN stands on his front lawn in the rain and wind. He is wearing a sling on his arm and looking at a Barbary Blackbird armband in his hand, a souvenir from the fight. It is late at night and the scene is reminiscent of the story's opening.

MARLIN (V.O.) (CONT'D)

That was three weeks ago, but it only seems like yesterday. The Barbary Blackbirds have literally disbanded. And for the present, things are quiet. I'm still recovering from my injuries and from the memory of that awful night. Some people say I was crazy, some say I was lucky. I say, I'm just a guy trying to get through another rainy night.

(beat)

Only tonight, the rain's got company.

The shot widens to reveal B.C. standing in the rain and the wind at MARLIN'S side. They turn and face each other. MARLIN takes off his fedora and puts it on B.C..

THE END

JACK MARLIN will return in . . . The Pretty One.

This MONTAGE is an excerpt from the sequel and is entitled JACK MARLIN AND THE PRETTY ONE. The sequel tells what happens to Toby after he mysteriously disappears at the end of JACK MARLIN, PRIVATE EYE: THE CASE OF THE BARBARY BLACKBIRD.

MONTAGE

INT. INSIDE MINE – NIGHT

1) The DUCE'S identity as a goblin has been revealed, the statue of the Barbary Blackbird knocked over, and pandemonium is ensuing in the cave. TOBY looks around at the confusion. He has taken a beating from Marlin and is somewhat disoriented.

2) He is now confronted with the knowledge of DUCE'S real identity. His eyes well up with tears of anger and betrayal. He clenches his fists, looks behind him at the gnomes, goblins, and trolls fleeing into the deeper recesses of the cave and decides to follow the gnomes headed for the exit.

3) TOBY is one of the last to leave. Part way down the passage, he stumbles and falls flat on his face when a group of panicked gnomes holding torches rush past him. He quickly struggles to get up.

TOBY

(desperately, weakly)

Wait! Wait!

SFX: FEARFUL, MUFFLED VOICES GROWING FAINT

4) TOBY manages to stand by clawing at the cave wall. The light in the distance is quickly fading; the voices of the fleeing gnomes are muffled and no one heeds his call. He reaches in his pocket for his lighter. Guided by its tiny flame, he gropes along the cave wall in what he believes to be the direction of the exit.

5) In his confusion, TOBY takes a turn that leads him to the underground cathedral rather than the mine exit. He enters the cathedral but in the darkness and his confusion, he does not notice its beauty or grandeur, rather he becomes afraid when he realizes he has taken a different path.

TOBY

(looking towards the ceiling)

I'm lost.

6) TOBY stumbles through the cathedral. He no longer needs his lighter since the cavern is lit by shadowy grey moonlight filtering through the openings in the ceiling. Rather than observe the cave's naturally formed stone columns and polished surfaces, he sees only ominous shapes and shadows looming up before him in the sparse moonlight.

7) He crosses the expanse and is able to make out an exit on the other side. He leaves the cathedral and makes his way along another path. After a short walk, he sees a defused light in the distance. He arrives at the entrance of ANTHONY'S study.

8) Peering through the entrance, TOBY sees a colossal dragon wearing a silk smoking jacket and sitting before a fireplace apparently engrossed in reading. Next to him on a small round table is a pipe resting against an ashtray and beside it a teacup and saucer.

9) TOBY tries to steady his legs. He is now a shadow of his former well-groomed self. His hair is standing up on his head from under his crumpled gnome cap; his clothes are torn and dirty; he has a black eye and his face is tear and dirt stained. He leans against the entrance straining his eyes in order to make out the figure who addresses him.

ANTHONY

(casually looking over his pince-nez)

Hello Toby. Who'd you steal the red hair from, your moth-er or your father?

10) TOBY is able to momentarily focus on ANTHONY, then collapses in the doorway.

END MONTAGE

GLOSSARY OF WORDS AND PHRASES

A little bird told me – source of information

Act casual – act as if one has nothing to hide

Angle – intention or agenda

Art Deco – designs noted for their stylized forms

At the bottom of things – find the truth

Blow one's cover – to be exposed or found out

Brazier – container for fire

Bud – short for buddy, man

Cable car – streetcar powered by cables in the pavement

Call a couple of the boys – ask for help

Can it – stop talking

Cathedral – grand building intended for worship

City infrastructure – a city's buildings and services

City park – park approximately the size of a city block

Chip off the old block – to be just like someone else

Copper – policeman

Countenance – facial expression

Crack a safe – rob a safe

Crack the case – solve the problem

Cross the line – go too far, break the law

Cul de sac – dead-end street

Cult – extraordinary beliefs and practices

Cut the chatter – stop talking

Dame – woman

Dead ringer – duplicate

Demeanor – appearance, bearing

Deodara – cedar pine

Destiny – future fate

Dick – detective

Disheveled – rumpled

Dispatch – notify by radio or mail

Dog one like a bad penny – person or idea that shows up often

Dope – information

Dough – money

Dupe – idiot

Earn one's stripes – achieve one's goal, accomplishment

Exhilaration – happiness

Explicatives – swear words

Fedora – stylish hat often worn by detectives

Ferry – boat used to cross a body of water

Flack – criticism, scolding

Flatfoot – policeman

Gargoyled – having the appearance of a gargoyle

Gatling gun – rapid repeating firearm

Get the upper hand – overcome, take charge

Give one the time of day – to give someone a chance

Gossamer silk – soft plant fibers or cobwebs

Gravity train – railroad cars powered by the force of gravity

Gut – stomach

Head of the clan – leader of a group of the same ancestry

Heating up – becoming more intense, exciting

Hideout – place to hide

Hideous – ugly

How do you figure? – what do you mean?

Inadvertently – not meaning to, unintentionally

Instincts – to have a sense of something, a hunch

Interrogated – asked questions

Job – robbery

Junk – typically a small Chinese fishing boat

Keep a cover on – watch out for or keep secret

Keep under wraps – to keep hidden

Knock over – rob

Knothole peeper – play on keyhole peeper, detective

Lay off – leave alone

Lie low – to keep out of sight

Lady Diana – leading lady Agnes Ayres in <u>The Sheik</u> (1921)

Leader of the pack – gang leader

Lookout – observer

Mac – name applied to an unknown man, insult

Maxfield Parrish – American Fantasy Painter and Illustrator.

Mom-and-pop grocery store – small family owned business

Mother hen – nurturing person

Mr. Moto – famous fictional Japanese detective

Mug/Mugs – criminal

Nab/Nabbed – take captive

Nail – catch someone in the act of committing a crime

Neck of the woods – familiar territory

Onyx – semiprecious black stone

Own up – admit, confess

Peeper – detective

P.I. – private investigator, detective

Pince nez – spectacles that clip on the nose

Play fair – honest

Playing from a marked deck – cheat

Presidio – former San Francisco military post

Put up to it – instigate or manipulate

Rabblerousing – incite people to riot or rebel

Raid the nest – clear out criminal activity

Renegade – lawbreaker

Retreat – place of rest and relaxation

Riffraff – criminal class

Ruckus – confusion, chaos

Rough up – beat up

Run a tight ship – well organized

Running board – long narrow step attached to a car

San Francisco Mint – building in which coins are manufactured

Sapshoe – play on gumshoe, detective

Shamus – detective

Shanghai – to force a person to board a ship bound for China

Shoot – talk

Significance – the importance of something

Silver Fizz – drink made with gin

Sinister – evil

Sister – woman

Slug/Slugged – punch

Snoop/Snooper – detective

Sock on the jaw – punch on the jaw

Socrates – Greek philosopher committed to the search for Truth

Song/to Sing – information or to relay information

Spunk – spirit, enthusiasm

Squeal/Squealed – to tell on someone

Stake out the neighborhood – police surveilance

Stay in touch – stay in contact

Sting – devise a plan to catch someone

Strait – reference to the Golden Gate Strait

Stow/Stowed – hide

Surveillance – watch

Svelte – slim and shapely

Take one out – restrain or put out of action

Take the gamble – take a chance

Tankard – a large cup or mug with a handle

The real McCoy – genuine

The same again – drink refill

Tip-off – give information

Tight ship – well organized

Trench coat – belted rain coat often worn by detectives

Trailed – followed

Trolley – electric powered San Francisco streetcar

Unexamined life – the life of a dull-witted or foolish person

Upscale digs – expensive apartment or residence

Valentino – Hollywood leading man in The Sheik (1921)

Wally/Wallies – Australian slang term for idiot

Wave of petty crime – series of small crimes

Weak-minded – stupid

Wellbeing – at peace

Yapping – talking

ANNOTATED LIST OF SELECTED WORKS

If some of the entries in the list of selected works seem unrelated, it is because the list was compiled specifically for use by the animators, storyboard artists, directors and producers in order to familiarize them with the persons, places, and sentiments that inspired the creation of the screenplay. A fuller justification for the works presented in this list is given in the accompanying film production suggestion guide (available from the author).

BOOKS
(Art Deco)

Bayer, Patricia. <u>Art Deco Source Book</u>. New Jersey: Wellfleet Press, 1988. A compendium of illustrations of architecture, furniture, sculpture, jewelry, and art objects from the Art Deco period.

Weber, Eva. <u>American Art Deco</u>. PA: JG P, 2004. A comprehensive work that includes 12x14 glossy pictures of Art Deco architecture, furniture, and a variety of art objects.

(San Francisco)

Asbury, Herbert. <u>The Barbary Coast: An Informal History of the San Francisco Underworld</u>. New York: Garden City Publishing Company, Inc., 1933. In a chapter entitled "'God Help the Poor Sailor!'", the author gives a detailed historical account of the how sailors were "shanghaied" in the days of the Barbary Coast.

Cameron, Robert, and Arthur Hoppe. <u>Above San Francisco</u>. San Francisco: Cameron and Company, 1998. Breathtaking color photographs of aerial views over San Francisco, the Golden Gate Strait, and Marin County. A weakness in the text, however, is the absence of nighttime aerial views over the City.

Doss, Margot, Patterson. <u>San Francisco at Your Feet: Great Walks in a Walker's Town</u>. New York: Grove Press, Inc. 1974. A concise, b/w illustrated guide to various sites of interest.

Garvey, John. <u>San Francisco Police Department</u>. Charleston, South Carolina: Arcadia, 2004. Part of the <u>Images of America Collection</u>, this volume contains numerous photos of officers from various eras in uniform and on the beat.

Richards, Rand. <u>Historic San Francisco: A Concise History and Guide</u>. San Francisco: Heritage House Publishers, 1991. A b/w illustrated history that provides an overview of the sites, history, and who's who.

—. <u>Historic Walks in San Francisco: 18 Trails through the City's Past</u>. San Francisco: Heritage House Publishers, 2002. A b/w illustrated walking guide to selected sites and some of the famous figures associated with them.

Wiley, Peter, Booth. <u>National Trust Guide San Francisco: America's Guide for Architecture and History Travelers</u>. New York: John Wiley & Sons, Inc., 2000. A b/w illustrated guide to San Francisco history, architecture, and walking tours.

(Detective / Mystery / Thriller)

Chandler, Raymond. <u>Stories and Early Novels</u>. New York: The Library of America, 1995. Contains pulp stories and popular novels, a chronology, and notes on texts.

—. <u>Later Novels and Other Writings</u>. New York: The Library of America, 1995. An anthology containing novels, selected essays and letters.

—. <u>Collected Stories</u>. New York: Everyman's Library, 2002. A wieldy volume containing all of Chandler's short fiction.

—. <u>Philip Marlowe's Guide to Life</u>. Ed. Martin Asher. New York: Alfred A. Knopf,2005. Some of Marlowe's best-known sayings, quips, and words of wisdom.

—. <u>Raymond Chandler Speaking</u>. Eds. Dorothy Gardiner and Kathrine Sorley Walker. Berkeley: University of California Press, 1997. Collection of Chandler's writings on various subjects taken primarily from his letters. Includes a few photos.

—. <u>Selected Letters of Raymond Chandler</u>. Ed. Frank McShane. New York: A Delta Book, 1987. A prolific and erudite letter writer, Chandler's correspondence covers a variety of topics. The Philip Marlowe material is especially interesting.

Collins, Max Allan. <u>The History of Mystery</u>. Portland: Collectors Press, 2001. An amazing archival work filled with detective history and illustrations spanning from the late 1700's to the present day.

Dubose, Martha Hailey. <u>Women of Mystery: The Lives and Works of Notable Women Crime Novelists</u>. New York: Thomas Dunne Books, 2000. Contains a fascinating exploration of Raymond' Chandler's critique of Golden Age detective fiction.

Durham, Philip. <u>Down These Mean Streets a Man Must Go</u>. Chapel Hill: University of North Carolina Press, 1963. In reference to Philip Marlowe, Durham writes, "Chandler brought together in one personification a representative folk hero; a combination of American frontier hero, war hero, political hero, athletic hero, and chivalric hero. Although he was only a symbol—albeit a symbol of honor in all things—Raymond Chandler's knight went among the people in the language of the people" (147).

Moss, Robert F. ed. <u>Raymond Chandler: A Literary Reference</u>. New York: Carroll and Graf Publishers, 2002. A must for serious Chandler scholars. In an excerpt taken from Philip Durham's <u>Down these Mean Streets a Man Must Go: Raymond Chandler's Knight</u> (1963), Durham quotes Chandler's description of Philip Marlowe, "But down these mean streets a man must go who is not himself mean, who is neither tarnished nor afraid. [. . .] He is the hero; he is everything. He must be a complete man and a common man and yet an unusual man.

He must be, to use a rather weathered phrase, a man of honor—by instinct, by inevitability, without thought of it, and certainly without saying it. He must be the best man in the world and a good enough man for any world. I do not care much about his private life; he is neither a eunuch nor a satyr; I think he might seduce a duchess and I am quite sure he would not spoil a virgin; if he is a man of honor in one thing, he is that in all things (283).

Nick Carter, Detective: Solution of a Remarkable Case (1891). By a Celebrated Author. Nick Carter Detective Library, No. 1. New York: Smith and Street, n.d. 4 July 2004 <http://www.sul.standford.edu/ depts/dp/ pennies/texts/ carter 1/_toc.html>. A Wonderful example of a Penny Dreadful (Dime Novel). The Stanford online collection is both scholarly and entertaining—a little gem for lovers of the genre.

Steinbrunner, Chris, and Otto Penzler. Encyclopedia of Mystery and Detection. New York: McGraw-Hill, 1976. As the title states, the work is an illustrated encyclopedic reference covering detective characters, authors, films, television, radio, plays, comics and books.

(Fantasy / Myth)

Barker, Cicely Mary. Flower Fairies of the Summer. London and Glasgow: Blackie, 1923. A small volume containing poems and pictures of fairies. The author was a homeschooled, self-taught artist whose illustrations of fairies portray them as graceful, untamed creatures devoid of guile or provocativeness.

Graham, Kenneth. "The Reluctant Dragon." Dream Days. 1902. 1 Jan. 2004 <http://www.gutenberg.org/dirs/etext95/ drday10.txt>. The story of a sophisticated, friendly dragon who has a keen appreciation for the finer things in life such as reciting poetry and art.

Huygen, Wil, and Rien Poortvliet. Gnomes. New York: Peacock Press, 1996. Considered by some to be the definitive book on the bearded and booted variety of gnomes.

Lewis, C. S. <u>Perelandra</u>. 1944. New York: Macmillan Co., 1972. The author's vivid description of the battle between Ransom and Weston, the Un-man, will remain fresh in the reader's mind long after the book is finished as will his description of Ransom's subterranean journey.

Lewis, C. S. <u>The Silver Chair</u>. 1953. New York: HarperTrophy, 2000. Contains detailed descriptions of a unique subterranean world and its inhabitants.

<u>The Maxfield Parrish Poster Book</u>. Intro. Alma M. Gilbert. San Francisco: Pomegranate Calendars and Books, 1989. Contains exquisite illustrations, particularly, <u>Waterfall</u>, 1930, p. 27 and <u>Contentment</u>, 1927, p. 55.

(ARTICLES / WEBSITES / MAPS / PHOTOS / ILLUSTRATIONS)

Huygen, Wil, and Rien Poortvliet. <u>Gnomes</u>. New York: Peacock Press, 1996. Introduction includes a map of sites where gnomes are reported to exist throughout North America.

<u>Map of California Historic Gold Mines</u>. California Geological Survey. 31 Dec. 2008 <http://www.consrv.ca.gov/cgs/geologic_resources/mineral_production/Documents/Big_AUMap.pdf>. Identifies the location of an abandoned lode mine near Muir Woods.

<u>Funimag</u>. Mount Tamalpais & Muir Woods Railway Traces. 31 Dec.2008 <http://www.funimag.com/photoblog/index.php/categorie/gravity-railroad/>. This site features archival photographs and video clips of a gravity train ride filmed by Thomas Edison on March 10, 1898. By 1930, the train was no longer in use.

"Twists, Slugs and Roscoes: A Glossary of Hardboiled Slang." Compiled by William Denton, 2005, Miskatonic U, 18 Jan. 2009 <http://www.miskatonic.org/slang.html>. Handy reference guide for terms commonly used during the 1930's.

RECORDINGS

Chandler, Raymond. <u>The High Window</u>. 1942. Read by Elliott Gould. Audiocassette. Dove Books on Tape, Inc., 1988

—. <u>The Mandarin Jade</u>. 1937. Read by Elliott Gould. CD. Audio Literature, 1996.

RADIO

<u>The Adventures of Philip Marlowe</u>. 1947-1951. Perf. Gerald Mohr. 92 shows. MP3 CD. OTRCAT.com, n.d. A thrilling series of broadcasts that can be listened to over and over again, and although financially lucrative, Chandler did not believe that the radio adaptations did his character justice. Truth to tell, however Gerald Mohr does one of the best Marlowe voice interpretations.

Raymond Chandler in conversation with Ian Fleming. "The Art of Writing Thrillers." BBC Radio. 10 July 1958. A discussion between two erudite men of the world whose writings have consistently affirmed what it means to be a person of honor living in a world where the relationship between honor and ethics is rarely understood.

FILM

Boothe, Powers, perf. <u>Philip Marlowe</u>. Dirs. Robert Iscove and Peter R. Hunt. 1986. 11 episodes. DVD. Goldhil Media, 2004. If ever there was an actor that could make one believe that Raymond Chandler's Philip Marlowe really exists, Powers Boothe is it. He outranks Mitchum, Bogart, Garner and others both in appearance and in his approach to the role.

<u>Danger Man</u>. Dirs. Julian Amyes and Terry Bishop. Perf. Patrick McGoohan. 1961. Complete First Season, 39 episodes. DVD. A&E, 2003. In his role as John Drake, McGoohan exemplifies the image of the lone hero—a man of few words who prefers a clean fight, his fists to a gun, and a good smoke to a roll in the hay. McGoohan is at his comedic best in The "Lonely Chair" episode.

Detectives 10 Pack. Perf. Basil Rathbone, Nigel Watson, Peter Lorre, Ray Milland, Ralph Byrd, Morgan Conway. 1930's. DVD. Mill Creek Entertainment, 2005. Selected film adaptations of comic strip characters and well known personalities from Literature. The Dick Tracy detective character played by actors Ralph Byrd and Morgan Conway do not have the suavity or believability of a Philip Marlowe, yet they are passable when compared to more recent caricatures.

Mr. Moto's Last Warning. Dir. Norman Foster. Perf. Peter Lorre. 1931. DVD. Alpha Video, 2002. One might forgive Mr. Moto's stereotypical coke-bottle spectacles, but not the prosthetic teeth. And in spite of Lorre's appeal as a mild-mannered Japanese detective, his Mr. Moto films remain an ideal example of why artists should carefully examine their justification for caricaturing or stereotyping people of different nationalities. In a world where history inevitably repeats itself and individuals are so easily seduced by prejudice, it is better not to feed that infernal fire. As in the case of the Charlie Chan films, the Moto material clearly draws on America's passion for the detective genre in a variety of guises.

Mr. Wong in Chinatown. Dir. William Nigh. Perf. Boris Karloff, Grant Withers. 1939. DVD. Alpha Video, 2002. The Mr. Wong series, including The Mystery of Mr. Wong, Doomed to Die, The Fatal Hour, and Mr. Wong Detective, are detective film classics. Karloff plays the character of Wong with savvy and sensitivity – a refreshing departure for viewers who only know him from his horror films. The material captures some of the views and mores of San Francisco during the 30's and 40's.

Out of the Past. Dir. Jacques Tourneur. Perf. Robert Mitchum. 1947. Videocassette. Turner Home Entertainment, 1990. A dark film with an unhappy ending; however, Mitchum in a fedora and trench coat walking the streets of San Francisco is a sight not to be missed.

Peter Gunn. Prod. Blake Edwards. Perf. Craig Stevens, Lola Albright, Herschel Bernardi, Hope Emerson. 1958-1959. Set 1, 16 episodes. DVD. A&E, 2002. Although Gunn (Craig Stevens) frequently fails to save his clients from being murdered, the series has a strong appeal arising mainly from the performances given by Albright (Edie Hart), Herschel (Lt. Jacoby) and Hope Emerson (Mother). The music of Henry Mancini makes this series a must for home film collections.

Phantom of Chinatown. Dir. Phil Rosen. Perf. Key Luke, Grant Withers. 1940. DVD. Alpha Video, 2003. Luke brings a new dimension to the role of Mr. Wong (at last, a Chinese detective hero being played by a Chinese actor), yet he may have been too young for the part, especially in the minds of Wong fans enamored of the Karloff material.

Marlowe. Dir. Paul Bogart. Perf. James Garner. 1969. Videocassette. MGM, 1994. A great Philip Marlowe parody. Contains a classic view of the inside of Marlowe's office.

The Big Sleep. Dir. Howard Hawks. Perf. Humphrey Bogart, Lauren Bacall. 1946. DVD. Warner, 2000. A hard hitting, no-nonsense portrayal of Chandler's Marlowe by Humphrey Bogart. The film is made rather heavy by its adult theme.

The Shanghai Cobra. Dir. Phil Karlson. Perf. Sidney Toler, Benson Fong, Mantan Moreland. 1945. DVD. MGM, 2004. In spite of the use of a non-Asian actor to play Charlie Chan, unforgivable racial stereotyping, and too much silly shtick, the Charlie Chan films including The Secret Service, The Jade Mask, Meeting at Midnight, The Chinese Cat, and The Scarlet Clue are to be commended for giving lead roles to Toler as the Chinese hero, his son (Fong) and African American manservant (Moreland) while drawing on America's passion for the detective genre.

Hama, Mie, perf. You Only Live Twice. Dir. Lewis Gilbert. 1967. Videocassette, MGM / UA, n.d. A wonderful performance by Mie Hama as Kissy Suzuki.

(Fantasy / Myth)

The Silver Chair. Dir. Alex Kirby. Perf. David Thwaites, Camilla Power, Richard Henders, Tom Baker. Videocassette. Bridgestone Multimedia, 1990. An outstanding adaptation of Lewis' work.

Interesting handling of the subterranean scenes and underground creatures.

Thunderbirds. Created by Gerry Anderson. Dirs. Brian Burgess and David Elliott. 1965. 12 volume complete set. DVD. A&E, 2002. A work of genius—the perfect combination of savvy, action, adventure, and ethics.

(Documentaries)

"Curse on the Gypsies." Narr. David Ackroyd. Writ. and Dir. Melissa Jo Peltier. History International Channel. 2 Jan. 2005. Eye-opening historical account of the Romany people.

"Most Haunted: Shanghai Tunnel." Narr. Michael Jones. Travel Channel. n.d. The segment provides an historical, though sensationalized, dramatization of a horrific chapter in US History.

ADDITIONAL WORKS

Dante, Alighieri. The Divine Comedy. Trans. Dorothy L. Sayers.3 vols. London: Penguin Books, 1949, 1955, 1962. In addition to the merits of the work itself, Sayers' brilliant translation and commentary makes these 3 volumes a must for every home library. *Il Purgatorio* and *L' Inferno* contain some thought-provoking scenes dealing with the subject of freewill, choice and consequence.

Loren, Sophia, perf. Yesterday, Today, and Tommorrow. Dir. Vittorio De Sica. 1964. Videocassette. Global Media, n.d. Sophia Loren is unparalleled in her performance as Adelina Sbaratti—*Molto Bella*!

Miner, Brad. The Compleat Gentleman: The Modern Man's Guide to Chivalry. Dallas: Spence Publishing Co., 2004. Miner writes, "If we are to have chivalry at all in a democratic age, we must reunite the concept with the sword it is meant to wield. Elegance alone will not suffice. A debonair man who is not also dangerous cannot be chivalrous. To say that the compleat gentleman is strong is to suggest two things: it is to evoke the ancient chivalric principle of prowess and to invoke the indispensability of self-discipline.

Among all the things a chivalrous man must be, this quality will probably be the most difficult for many to accept. . . . He must, however, possess a *martial spirit*" (186). Miner also believes that women can espouse these same virtues as well as possess martial capabilities. Of *sprezzatura*, the author says, it is a term that can characterize a gentleman's conduct of life. "A man [woman] who has *sprezzatura* is a man content to keep his own counsel. He not only does not need to have his motives understood; he prefers that they *not* be understood. His actions, including his carefully chosen words, speak for him. . . . He is like a warrior, because he knows that there are things worth fighting for and will fight. He is a lover, because he allows his wife and family to liberate him from the tyranny of ego. He is like a monk, because he employs learning to unlock the mysteries of the human heart. He [She] is possessed of that commingling of restraint and detachment that is *sprezzatura* and that we can as easily call *cool*" (227, 236).

Miner, Brad. Interview with Raymond Arroyo. "The Compleat Gentleman." <u>The World Over</u>. Videocassette. EWTN. Irondale Alabama. 24 Sept. 2004. Miner gives a brilliant overview of his masterwork <u>The Compleat Gentleman</u>.

Milton, John. <u>Paradise Lost</u>. New York: Holt, Rinehart and Winston, Inc., 1951. In addition to its many merits, this epic poem is a good reference for battle scenes and subterranean realms.

Nelson, Victoria. "Rosemary Sutcliff's Arthurian Trilogy." <u>Saint Austin Review</u> 2.11 (December 2002): 10-14. A close examination of Sutcliff's retelling of the Arthurian tales and how they reflect, in Suttcliff's own words, that "Doing the right / kind / brave / honest thing doesn't have to result in any concrete reward [. . .] and that this doesn't matter; the reward lies in having done the right / kind / brave / honest thing, in having kept faith with one's own integrity—and probably in being given a more difficult thing to do next time" (10).

Nelson, Victoria. "Teaching Ian Fleming's James Bond Novels from a Catholic Perspective." <u>Saint Austin Review</u> 8.3 (May/June 2008):

8-12. Posits a clear-cut argument for the Bond novels as Literature using excerpts from the various texts together with Fleming's own thoughts on writing as well as references to similar narratives by C. S. Lewis, Walker Percy, and Rider Haggard—authors whose works are already considered by many to be part of the cannon of classical Literature. Of Fleming's works, Nelson writes, "The Bond narratives reveal the ongoing struggle to overcome the power of evil and how, in the process, the limits of human freedom are constantly being tested".

Star Wars: The Power of Myth. New York: D.K., 1999. Every home library should contain a copy of this profusely illustrated, philosophical, scholarly work.

The Sheik. Dir. George Melford. Perf. Rudolph Valentino, Agnes Ayres. 1921. DVD. Image, 2002. The Sheik (Valentino) and his Lady Diana (Ayres) remain as strong an icon for anguished passion and romance today as when they first appeared onscreen together eighty-five years ago.

ABOUT THE AUTHOR

VICTORIA NELSON is a freelance writer from California who holds an MA in English Literature from Holy Names University. She is a writing tutor for graduate students and a homeschool curriculum consultant. Other publications include a stage play, *L. is for Sayers,* and a novel, *Romana Volume I From the Annals of Romana.* She is also a contributing author to the *Saint Austin Review (StAR).*

www.ingramcontent.com/pod-product-compliance
Lightning Source LLC
Chambersburg PA
CBHW071305130626
46556CB00003B/1474